Deryn Pittar is an award-winning author, who writes Sci-Fi, fantasy, futuristic and contemporary fiction, plus a dash of horror. She enjoys the challenge of short and flash fiction and dabbles in poetry. She is published in many genres, including poetry.

The Carbonite's Daughter, a dystopian novel, was published in 2022 by IFWG Australia. The sequel, *Quake City* was released in 2024.

Quake City

by
Deryn Pittar

This is a work of fiction. The events and characters portrayed herein are imaginary and are not intended to refer to specific places, events or living persons. The opinions expressed in this manuscript are solely the opinions of the author and do not necessarily represent the opinions of the publisher.

Quake City

All Rights Reserved

ISBN-13: 978-1-922856-83-8

Copyright ©2024 Deryn Pittar

V1.1

This book may not be reproduced, transmitted, or stored in whole or in part by any means, including graphic, electronic, or mechanical without the express written consent of the publisher except in the case of brief quotations embodied in critical articles and reviews.

IFWG Publishing International
Gold Coast

www.ifwgpublishing.com

For my family. Thank you for your unfailing support and belief in my ability.

Chapter 1

The aftershocks continued to rattle the earth, vibrating under Calista's feet. The dawn breeze picked up the dust and swirled it into tiny tornadoes that raced a short way and collapsed back to the ground. She dragged her gaze away from the distant mountains, broken and scarred by the horrific earthquakes of the past hour. This line of peaks, riddled with tunnels in which they had lived and now escaped from, must surely have shattered inside. She turned to look to the wagon they were following and to the future that lay in front of them.

The weary group of adults, teenagers and children, perhaps twenty-five in total, had, with Mathew's guidance, slowly worked their way down the mountainside in the dark to the wagon that waited at the bottom.

Lack of sleep prickled the back of her eyes and she reached for Mathew's hand as they slipped on the gravel down the slope to the dry riverbed. In a few weeks the spring thaw would fill it with snow-melt, but at present the wagon jolted over the smooth stones. One child, still awake, giggled at the new experience.

A low, distant rumble grew to a roar. The earth groaned and bucked, another earthquake struck. She gripped Mathew's hand to prevent herself from falling onto the stones and doubted her hearing as the earth gurgled.

"Liquefaction!" shouted Winston. "We have to get out of here." The ground rolled and grumbled as if wanting to open beneath them. The wagon rocked as the stones in the river course seethed and rattled. The sand between the stones frothed, and bubbles formed and burst. Mathew dropped her hand.

"Hurry," he shouted, and ran past the stragglers and the wagon to the front of the shafts where he reached and held the horse's bridle.

Winston slapped the reins on Buster's back and shouted, "Mathew, get back." When Buster didn't move fast enough, Winston pulled a whip from under the seat and snapped it next to the horse's ears. "Watch the children," he yelled over his shoulder, and the grandparents on the wagon sprawled across the sleeping children to hold them still and stop them sliding off the back.

With no previous experience of earthquakes, the tunnel dwellers were gripped with fear, and they stood paralysed in the middle of the dry river course. The horse trembled within the shafts of the wagon and neighed loudly. His squeals of terror only served to frighten the escapees even more.

The earth continued to roll and grumble beneath their feet, and Calista looked down to see a watery sludge bubbling and oozing between the rocks.

"Get behind the wagon," Mathew yelled, pointing at the men in the party who were now moving, having overcome their fear.

"Push," shouted Winston, "We have to get out of the river bed."

His orders brooked no argument. The women scattered and scrambled toward higher ground. The men rushed to the back of the cart. Winston slapped the reins on Buster's back and shouted. This time he whipped the horse's rump.

Calista had never seen him treat the horse in this manner. Down around the wagon's wheels, slurry bubbled like a boiling mud pool, but there wasn't any steam. This water had risen from the depths, and it splashed cold against her legs when she jumped across the stones.

The horse tried again to move forward but the wagon held, the wheels clasped in the rising liquefaction. "Push, everyone. Shout to encourage the horse." Winston snapped the whip again. "Come on, Buster. Pull, boy, pull," The animal appeared to overcome its terror and with a mighty leap wrenched the wagon wheels free. The deck dipped and rocked until the wagon reached the bank. The grandparents on the wagon held the mattresses firm, their arms securing the children while the horse pulled the wagon through the well-worn track to higher ground, away from the grasping mud. Standing on the firm surface, Buster trembled and neighed with distress. The earth's protests quietened to a slow rumble which heaved through the countryside in waves, shaking bushes, bending the sparsely scattered trees, causing stones to roll and dust eddies to rise.

Mathew held the horse, talking to Buster in soothing tones, while Winston climbed down and checked the wagon wheels. The adults, having scrambled to safety, gathered in a group. Fear had sapped their energy and lined their faces.

For these recently-escaped inhabitants of the Erewhon community the earthquakes of the past hour were terrifying. Even being out in the open was a new experience. Everything must seem strange, and Calista remembered her own awe and apprehension when she'd first ventured outside. It'd been a mere six months ago, yet it seemed like an age because so much had happened since that first day when she'd followed her father down the mountainside and met his band of followers, the Carbonites.

After being up all night, everybody succumbed to their weariness this morning and slowly the group sank to the ground. The children in the back of the wagon remained asleep, catching up on the rest they'd missed. The excitement of liberty, the freedom to run around in ever-widening circles when they'd stopped for an early morning meal, had added to their exhaustion. Calista checked on Caleb, Vanily and the other youngsters, then joined the group to reassure the parents their children were fine.

"They've slept through it all," she said with a grin. "I think it would take a clap of thunder to wake them."

"Last time I heard a clap of thunder I was in Wanaka on health leave," Pelly said, "Not that it made me any healthier. I nearly died of fright."

There were a couple of half-hearted laughs, but there was an element of truth in Pelly's comment. You had to be outside to hear thunder. Calista reckoned it would frighten every one of the travellers even after the roar of the earthquakes. Within the tunnels, the sound of the generators and air conditioning units had drowned out other noises, the loudest noise of all being the train as it rumbled through the station on its way south or north twice a day.

After the first earthquake over an hour before, they had all chattered with relief, glad to be out of the Southern Alps and in the open space of the Canterbury plains where nothing could fall on them. They'd watched the mountain range contort and roll in the dawn light, the quake shaking the snow-capped peaks bare and causing giant slabs of rock to slither down the mountainside to hit the ground, creating huge plumes of dust. Their previous home now possibly lay in ruins. One of the few positive outcomes of the destruction of their former home would be that pursuit by the Men in Charge—the MICs—would be highly unlikely. Their hands would be full administering the repair of the damage within the tunnels.

The journey down the mountain in the dark had been a great adventure for the children. The adults, just as exhausted and deprived, now trudged across the plains toward freedom and a new life without lies and indentured work, they hoped.

Mathew moved and stood beside Calista, and with his arm around her waist he hugged her tight.

"Are you alright?" He kissed her head as she leaned against him.

"We're just fine," she said, knowing he'd be concerned about the baby. It had only been an hour ago that she'd told him he was going to be a father. Perhaps she should have waited until they'd reached Castor Seville's farm. Now he would be worrying all the time and probably insist she ride the wagon instead of walking with the others.

Dr Webb stepped into the middle of the group and began what seemed to Calista to be a pep talk, designed to calm the fear she could faintly smell emanating from the weary travellers.

"What a lot of long faces." Dr Webb's voice was hearty and cheerful. "Here we are on a beautiful day—and we are outside! Look around you." He spread his arms and turned in a circle. "Open ground and space for as far as the eye can see. Isn't that wonderful?"

Most of the adults nodded, dredging smiles from the depth of their weary bodies.

In a softer tone he continued. "Thanks to Calista and Mathew we all escaped down the mountain, long before the first earthquake struck. How lucky is that? Then at the bottom we had Winston and Buster waiting for us with food and a ride for the children—and the grandparents," he added, grinning at the elderly couple who were stretching their limbs by walking around.

"I know you'll be worrying about family and friends left behind who might be injured, but I have a plan hatching about that. Besides, all the worry in the world won't make a damned bit of difference, now. One good thing about it is the MICs will have their hands too full to be bothered chasing after us."

There were a few chuckles about that and Calista noticed the other women in the group were now chatting amongst themselves, their backs straighter their smiles broad.

"What about the radiation, Dr Webb?" Samuel Hager's was looking about, brow creased, as if the radiation might be seen hovering in the air.

"That's everywhere, even in the tunnels, as Calista proved at the community meeting a few days ago when the lights went out. All of you here saw those members of the community who had developed 'Angel's Kiss'." Again heads nodded. "Some people seem to absorb radiation more readily than others, and when your body has too much it makes you hair glow in the dark."

"I'm having second thoughts about my decision to come along," Samuel admitted. "Is there more out here than in the tunnels?"

"I don't think so. I honestly don't know, but remember the MICs have been telling everyone for many years that there is no radiation in the tunnels and that we were all safe. Now we all know they were lying." He stepped closer to Samuel and grasped his shoulder. "Would you rather raise your family in the dark tunnels, or have them enjoy a life full of sunshine, rain and the occasional thunderstorm? I think you've made the right decision."

Samuel smiled and hugged his wife Rose. "Thank you, Dr Webb. I'm a bit of a worrywart at the best of times."

Rose nodded in agreement. "I'm glad we came," she said.

"Enough serious talk," Winston cajoled. "I've been outside for many years and I don't have 'Angel's Kiss'." He pointed to a spindly tree nearby. "There's a bit of shade here and I think it's time Buster had a rest."

Mathew fetched the food baskets from the back of the wagon while Winston unhitched the horse, tied him to a nearby bush and gave him oats in a nosebag. Buster would not normally wander away but should another quake roll through he could be frightened into bolting. That couldn't be risked: the horse and wagon were essential to their trip to the farm.

Calista helped Mathew unpack the food and listened to a nearby conversation between Jason Fletcher and Winston.

"What was that stuff in the riverbed?" Jason asked, scratching the stubble on his chin.

"That slurry is called liquefaction," Winston said. "It bubbles up during a quake when the water table is high, bringing sand with it." He pointed at the smooth riverbed which had been a rock-scattered hollow but was now a sand-filled dip where occasional bubbles erupted and burped. "It's like a sandy glue and once it dries out it sets like concrete. There's a swathe of it in Quake City. Places originally covered in liquefaction in 2011 have been built on. Personally, I think it's a crazy idea. What if it turns to glue again?"

"Does it happen every time there's an earthquake?"

"Don't think so. Mostly it's where there's a high water table. The 2011 Quake that killed so many people in Quake City wasn't very deep. This one"—he waved his arms about—"seems to be shallow as well. More of an aftershock than a real big shake; not like the one that broke the mountain range." He pointed to the Alps, where another dust cloud rose in the mid-morning sunshine as another rock-face crumbled to the mountain's baseline.

"It's all so strange to us. We've been tunnel dwellers all our lives." Jason pointed to the sky. "The sunshine is extra bright and the air is so crisp it almost feels as if it's cleaning your tubes as you breathe."

Winston laughed, "You'll soon get used to it. Wait till we get a snowstorm. Now that's a sight to behold."

"I'll look forward to that," Jason said, and with a nod of thanks picked up the two mugs of tea and carried them to his parents, who now stood with the group. Despite being the eldest people there, both had an air of strength about them as they surveyed their new world.

Nothing frail about those two, Calista decided, and thought of her mother's sudden retreat back into the tunnels, just when she'd reached the exit. Was she alive? Or had she been crushed in the quake? Surely by the time it struck she'd have safely returned to their apartment—but the living quarters may now lie in fractured pieces. Hadn't Dr Webb said all the services would probably have been destroyed? She banished the images of broken water pipes and naked electric wires. With a deep breath she strode to the wagon's side, checked once more on the sleeping children, and walked over to join Mathew and Dr Webb, who seemed to be having a serious discussion of their own.

"You can't go on your own," she heard Mathew say.

"But I have to go.' Dr Webb's voice trembled and his round face seemed to crumble into itself.

"Then I will go with you."

"Go? Where?" Calista queried as she stepped to Mathew's side. "Who's going where?"

The short silence should have warned her that the subject of their discussion was not going to please her.

"Dr Webb feels he should return to the mountain and look out for people who may have managed to escape." Mathew peered into the distance, back where they'd come from, as if he could see people fleeing down the Alps. Calista opened her mouth to protest but Mathew carried on. "I was telling Dr Webb that he couldn't go alone. It would be foolish to think he could climb back to Exit E5 and perhaps venture inside the tunnels without someone to help him and give support."

Keeping her anger to herself, Calista took a long deep breath before she spoke. "I can understand how you feel, Dr Webb, your Hippocratic oath alone would drive you to do this, but…" Now she really had to be diplomatic. "I have a suggestion." She put her hand on Mathew's shoulder and held his gaze. "How many hours have we been walking? Six?" He nodded. "And how many hours until we reach Castor Seville's farm?"

"About three hours, walking at our present pace." He looked toward the farm. He probably knew what she was going to suggest.

"If you walk back to the Alps now, it will take another six hours to return to the bottom of the path. By then you will have walked for twelve hours." She hurried on as her thoughts tumbled out. "You will be tired, with no food and shelter, and won't be able to do anything useful until tomorrow morning. Plus, neither of you have had any sleep for over twenty-four hours." She pointed to the west. "Why not carry on to the farm with us, rest for a few hours, get a couple of Castor's horses, maybe even a cart, and ride back at dawn. You can borrow ropes and axes to help you climb to Exit 5E. The path has fallen away in places. We saw it happen. Hopefully you can take food and a tent with you." She pointed to Dr Webb, "At present all you have between the two of you is one bag with medical supplies and two legs each." She shut her mouth tight before she added "utter madness" and waited for common sense to prevail. It took a few moments but then Dr Webb nodded.

"You're quite right, Calista; a totally sensible suggestion. My heart is ruling my head—again." He turned back to face the assembled group where everyone stood watching them, waiting to begin the last leg of the journey. "We'll do that, shall we, Mathew?"

Mathew nodded his agreement. "Yes, we'll need ropes and food if we are to be of any use. Besides, if anyone manages to get down the mountain today they will be on their way westward by tomorrow. There's no other direction to go really, except to come across the plains toward the coast, and we can guide them on to Castor's."

Dr. Webb's voice had firmed with enthusiasm. "Also, the people at Castor's will need to know there could be tunnelers on their way, looking for a safe haven and work perhaps. We will be able to tell them about the mountain moving when we get there."

Calista walked off, leaving the two men to follow. She climbed up onto the cart and murmured to Winston, "Let's get moving. We are all so tired. I can't wait to get there." This was a lie.

She feared seeing Castor Seville again after the advancements he'd made when she stayed with her father on the first night of freedom. Would he be as insistent, wanting her to become his wife and bear his children? He might even want to take Caleb and Vanily and claim them as his. She shuddered at the thought and then decided at their next rest stop she would talk to Mathew about how to handle Castor Seville. Mathew would have to stand beside her and claim her as his partner. That should stop the man's crazy plan.

He'd followed her and the Carbonites to Quake City hoping to convince her to be his wife, but her father had heard he'd arrived and instead of returning to the Stockade from the Ferrymead fair, they had climbed the Port hills "to look at the view". It had seemed odd to her at the time. They'd spent the night in a hotel, and she'd discovered later, it was all to avoid Castor Seville.

If he hadn't been such a generous supporter of the Carbonites, surely her father would have taken a firmer stand against Castor's desires. The surplus produce from his farm was the lifeblood of the Carbonites' good work in Quake City, and in the past few months she had come to realise how important Castor's generosity was to the survival and reasonable health of many people. Would she be forced to weigh the need of the Carbonites against her own needs and safety? The next few days could put this to the test; fear versus family—and now Mathew, who could protect her, intended to return to the tunnels.

Chapter 2

Refuelled and energised, their trek resumed with Mathew insisting she ride up front on the wagon next to Winston. Weariness chilled her and she pulled her cloak tight across her chest. The cloak rustled in her ears as it slithered up her neck, tucking itself into all her hollows, hugging her like the true friend it was. Her "magic" cloak, that Wallace Howe had given her when Caleb had been born. She'd always thought it was a gift from the MICs. Now she knew that Wallace Howe was the sperm donor of her two children. As much as she disliked Mr Howe, she didn't hold it against the cloak. It had kept her warm through all her travels, an irreplaceable gift.

The rocking of the wagon fatigued her and she leaned against Winston's shoulder, just for a moment, to ease her head, only to wake when the wagon halted.

"Rest stop," Winston called, and while he fed Buster some more oats, Mathew and Dr Webb handed out fruit and drink.

"Nearly there," Mathew said, and pointed to the white dot in the distance. "That's our goal, that house in the distance. There will be places to rest in the workers' accommodation and more food." He beamed at the struggle of tired people. "You've all done so well. You can sleep for two days once we get there."

"I think I will," said Mrs Grayson, a brave smile creasing her weary face, "As long as someone will look after April," Her daughter of six had slept on the wagon and was now racing around with the other children.

Calista noticed Pelly had her arm around young Peter Tonkin. His shoulders were shaking and Pelly was patting his back. Was he crying? She hurried over.

"Are you all right, Peter? What's the matter?"

He looked at her with red-rimmed eyes and wiped his sleeve across his tear-stained cheeks. "I guess it's just hit me that my folks might have been killed in the first big quake, or even in the smaller ones we've had since." He took a ragged breath. "The others…" He pointed to the other teenagers. "They all told their parents they were leaving, but I slid into the group at the exit, when Dr Webb asked me if I wanted to join all of you. It was a great idea and I'm happy I came, but my poor parents have no idea where I am. If they're alive they will be frantically looking for me." He wasn't very tall and a bit on the thin side, probably still growing. His gaze drifted to the far-off, snow-capped range. "And what about Fogarty, the guard that Winston tied up at the exit? He could still be bound up and no one has come to untie him. He wasn't a bad man, just following orders."

She'd forgotten about the guard they'd left tied up at the exit. Peter's guard's uniform looked tatty and creased out in the sunlight and the silver material had lost its shine in places. Whoever designed it must have watched Star Wars holograms. In the dim lights of the tunnel, it had been quite impressive. Now it looked silly.

"I think you should talk to Mathew and Dr Webb. Tomorrow morning, early, they are planning to take some horses, maybe even a cart, and return to the mountain. They'll need your help if you'd like to go with them. I'm sure they will be very grateful for a strong young man. You are just the right size to get around tight corners." She could imagine him crawling through tight places. She'd try and find him something else to wear before he left in the morning.

He straightened his slumped shoulders and managed a smile of thanks before he hurried over to join the two men.

An animated conversation had begun and Dr Webb's waving arms indicated plans were being hatched.

"Perhaps I should go too," Pelly said, and Calista's stomach developed a rock in it.

"Oh no, I need you, Pelly. Please don't go with them."

"You do?" The young girl's face lit as if no one had ever needed her before. Perhaps that's why she'd joined the group, to flee indifference.

"I'm being purely selfish, I know, but I've always worked and Mother looked after the children. I'm not very good at mothering, and you seem to be a natural."

Pelly grinned, "Yes, I like little kids."

"I don't mean you have to look after them all the time, but I'd appreciate your help." She could see Winston getting ready to move on. "Also, you should know that outside, a young girl like you, nice looking and healthy, will be sought after as a wife. Be warned and don't rush into a relationship too soon. Don't be surprised if you attract a lot of interest."

"Really?" Pelly's eyebrows rose. "That will be a first for me. The MICs didn't think I was breeding material."

"To hell with the MICs, and everyone like them" Calista cursed. "They no longer have any say about anything you and I do." She secretly hoped the three local MICs had been killed in their small fiefdom of Erewhon Station. It wasn't the right thing to think, so she didn't say it. There'd be lots of MICs alive in Wanaka and Queenstown, no doubt. The "Men in Charge" would have made sure they got the best and safest places to live.

She looked around. They were a tired and dusty lot. Lack of sleep had softened all their stances and weariness etched lines on everyone's faces. Yet, as they readied to begin the last section of their trek to freedom, an air of anticipation and excitement lightened their steps. On the western horizon, Castor Seville's huge double-storeyed mansion stood, presently a small white dot in the landscape.

Calista walked over and stood beside Mathew, tugged on his jacket and edged him away from the others. 'I need to talk," she said.

"Thought you might," he murmured, looking a bit shame-faced "I can't let the doctor go on his own, Callie. We need to go back and rescue who we can. Eleanor might be alive and shocked enough to come outside. Peter Tonkin wants to come too."

Calista waved his comments away, "I know all about Dr Webb's responsibilities and your lifetime of servitude as a Carbonite. I understand your need to help, but I'm more worried about arriving at the farm—and Castor Seville's reaction to seeing me again." Her lip trembled. "I'm quite frightened of him. He might want to keep my children."

Mathew wrapped her in his arms and kissed the top of her head. "Don't worry about him! I forgot to tell you, in all the excitement over the past few days. When Winston and I stopped there on the way to rescue you, Castor was in Quake City. The cook said he'd found a lady there who has agreed to marry him. He is supposed to be returning with his bride, any day now. I can't see him bothering you again." He ran his finger across her lips, "Come on, give me a smile. Life isn't that bad."

She managed a stiff smile. Castor Seville was a megalomaniac. One wife might not be enough to satisfy his ego. His visions of grandeur might include a harem. What if this woman was sterile? Nothing would stop him until he'd sired children and one child wouldn't be enough. To appease Mathew and hide her fear she added, "Thank heavens for that. At last, he has someone to breed with—and best of all, it's not me." The sooner she could get away from the farm and back in Quake City the safer she'd feel.

Again her gaze drifted to the far mountain range. Its snowy caps glistened in the sun, but the despair of the dim existence in its tunnels swamped her senses. She peered back over the plains they'd crossed today, looking for signs of pursuit. Parts of the escape path had collapsed; they'd seen it happen. Would this stop the MICs sending scouts to follow them? Without the path, perhaps they'd just slide down the mountain. The memories of her capture and return to the tunnels flashed into her mind, causing her to close her eyes, cutting out the view of the majestic Southern Alps which held so many sad memories.

Their arrival at the farm passed in a blur of shouts of welcome and farmhands offering to entertain the children, now wide awake and ready for adventure. The adults quaffed large mugs of hot drink and fresh scones before heading for beds and bunks in the workers' sleeping quarters. Calista vaguely remembered Mathew climbing into bed and to her murmured query he replied their rescue mission was all organised. With that, she slept until Mathew's early morning preparations woke her. In the dark they dressed, whispered to each other so as not to wake the children, and crept out to join the team of volunteers.

On the eastern horizon a slash of dawn light peeped through the brooding clouds. The rain was on its way and no doubt they'd all be wet within an hour or two. Not that the gathered group seemed dismayed. The last ten minutes had involved the checking of supplies and the harnesses on the two horses.

"So you're off, then?" Calista said as Mathew walked toward her for a final hug before they set off back to the cursed Southern Alps. "All checked and ready?" She knew her tone of voice wasn't pleasant. Finally, they were safe. She'd thwarted the MIC's plans for her and now, instead of hurrying home to Quake City, Mathew intended to go back into the mountain. It made her feel cheated of the euphoria she should be feeling. Perhaps she was just tired.

Over Mathew's shoulder stood the assembled rescue team, with provisions, ropes, a large tent rolled up on the back of one of the two wagons. Castor's foreman, Will Jasper, had loaned a total of six horses, four to ride and two to pull. A taciturn fellow, whose lined face brooked no argument, he'd insisted Mathew and Dr Webb take several of his men, mainly to guard the horses and wagons while they conducted their "fool's errand", as he put it, to climb the mountain to the exit and see if there were survivors.

"I've no truck with tunnelers," he'd said. "Soft, don't like hard physical work. Just want to sit around and eat." This had been accompanied by a glare toward the hungry travellers last evening, who'd cleared the table of the food Cook had provided. All were now sleeping off the strain of their journey across the plains.

Luckily, Jasper agreed to Dr Webb and Mathew's plans and despite his taciturn manner had organised everything they might need in the six hours the men had rested. She would thank him personally once the party departed. His gruff manner belied his good deeds. Perhaps it was just a front. He'd found some clothes for Peter Tonkin too, who looked more grown-up now he was out of his ridiculous guard's uniform.

Mathew kissed her gently, his lips warm against hers despite the cold morning. "You take care now," he whispered.

"It's going to rain. You should take my cloak."

He scoffed, "That cloak only responds to you. Last time I put it on it went as stiff as a board. I don't think it likes me. Besides, I have my felted jacket, pure wool, it will keep me dry." He was right. While her cloak would stretch to cover them both to keep them warm while sleeping, it would not behave normally if someone else tried to wear it. It seemed linked to her DNA, like a blood relative. One day someone might tell her what it was made of. Although she'd been told it was made of tyvek, like her overalls, she doubted this: her overalls had no personality at all.

Once the cavalcade has disappeared down the tree-lined driveway and out of sight, Calista turned and went looking for the foreman. She found him in the stables, giving directions to three workers about the day ahead and their allotted jobs. She waited at the door until he'd finished and stepped toward him as he came out.

"Mr Jasper, can I have a moment of your time?"

He stopped, his eyebrows raised and his head to the side. "Yes, Miss Waterman, what can I do for you?"

She took a slow breath, gathered her sleep-deprived thoughts and smiled. Most of all she needed this man's co-operation and approval.

"I'm aware of your opinion of tunnelers, sir, but I'd like to explain a few things." He nodded and she hurried on. "The three families that came out with us spent their lives serving their community, but they left behind everything they owned and everyone they knew to come here. They took a brave step to give their children a future, and I can assure you they are not layabouts or idle people." She shoved her trembling hands into the pockets of her overalls, to hide her nervousness. "Mr Hager worked as a water engineer so if there is anything you might need fixing in your irrigation system I am sure he could help and will do so willingly.

"Mr Fletcher, who brought his parents with him, is a general maintenance man and can turn his hand to fixing most things. He is also very good at making furniture, so if you have anything in the house that needs repairing or even wagon wheels that need fixing, I'm sure he would be delighted to help. I don't know what his parents' skills are but they are very sprightly for their age. They won't be a burden." By now the foreman's eyebrows had lowered and his lips pursed. He seemed interested in her story.

"Pelly worked in the hydroponic gardens with me and she is good with children. Mrs Grayson is a widow and has her young daughter with her. She was one of our teachers, and I seem to remember that you have a small school here for your workers' children. If you wanted her to help I'm sure she will." At this, Jasper nodded his approval.

"There are also several other teenagers: Peter Tonkins, who has gone with Mathew, and three teenage boys who have left their families for a big adventure. I'm sure they can work doing something. They're young and enthusiastic, even if they are not as strong as grown men."

"It all sounds very promising, Miss Calista."

"I know we will be here for a few days, Mr Jasper, and I want to assure you we will not take your hospitality for granted. As soon as we can we will move on to Quake City, but as you know"—she pointed to the west—"Mathew and the others will probably be gone for a few days. Until they return, we'll all pay our way with labour."

"And what about yourself?" There was a teasing tone in his voice and a wry smile played around his lips. "What can you do, other than breed?"

Surely he didn't know she was pregnant! No, he must be referring to her first arrival at the farm when her hair was in cornrows, the mark of a breeder. She would not let this man's pointed comment spur her into a sharp retort. She swallowed and answered in a calm, level tone, as if he had been civil and not snide. "I've worked in hydroponic gardens and I have some knowledge of herbal medicine that I learned from Dr Elizabeth when in Cheviot and inland in Parnassus. I'm also useful in the kitchen and intend to offer my services to your cook, Mrs Rasmussen."

"Daphne's mother, you mean?"

"I didn't know that."

"I'm sure Cook will be glad of a hand seeing as Daphne has been up all night, totally beside herself with so many youngsters to talk to, not to mention the young men." Again his voice carried his displeasure. "She will be of no use today at all."

"Then I'll see Mrs Rasmussen shortly after I have woken the others. They can begin their second day of freedom from the dim life they've had up to now." She ducked her head and resisted the urge to salute the man. He had that air of authority about him. He lifted his battered hat to her, murmured "Good day" and strode off in the direction of the mill.

Perhaps this time she'd get to see the flour mill and the waterwheel. Her promised tour had been cut short on her last visit, in her father's rush to get her away from Castor. Yes, she would need to wake the men, if not the women, and ask them to offer their services to the foreman. She would talk to the women after she'd been to see Cook.

She turned and walked to the accommodation block, rehearsing her talk to the others. Nothing really changed in life. This is exactly what they did in the tunnels, only now they could do it in the sunshine.

The sun's morning rays lit the dew. It sparkled like a scattering of fallen stars on the grass. She stopped to admire the miracle of a spider's web, hanging between two twigs and dressed in droplets. Her heart lifted and joy surged through her weary body.

It was so good to be outside again. She felt the brush of butterfly wings in her stomach. The baby had quickened, responding to her happiness.

Chapter 3

The climb to Exit E5 was worse than Mathew could ever imagine. For every three steps upward they slid back two. The gravel and rocks gave under their feet and their knees bore witness to the constant falls. Every rise above them they thought would be their last, only to be confronted by another hump to climb over. Finally, the path appeared and they rested on the narrow platform, regaining their breath and strength, before walking along the gentle rise to the exit doorway.

"I wonder if Mr Fogarty is still tied up?" Mathew said, between attempts to get his breath back. At least the journey down would be quicker.

"He'll be very cross if he is," Peter Tonkin commented. The young lad didn't seem the slightest out of breath and his grin displayed his enjoyment of their climb.

"We'll soon find out. If someone found him then there might be more guards on duty—or he might have gone inside to search for survivors," Dr Webb said. "It depends on his circumstances and whether he has family at risk. Either way, we'll know in a minute. Be prepared for trouble, Mathew."

Mathew wished he'd brought his bo with him, his Kenpo fighting stick, but there'd been a limit to what they could carry on the climb and he'd needed both his hands in places to hang onto thin bushes to prevent a backward slide until he found new footing. Even with it strapped on his back it could have tangled in the bushes as they climbed.

They paused at the entrance, assessing any hidden danger.

Mathew threw his arm out to stop Peter rushing forward.

The steel door stood ajar, one corner buried in the ground, and the warped frame would never allow it to be closed again. Just as well they'd left it open when they fled; otherwise, it would have been jammed shut by the quake and their rescue mission would have been impossible at this portal. It would have taken them another day to go down and climb again to the next exit. He peered into the dark tunnel, only able to see as far as the daylight carried, and scanned the rock floor and walls. They seemed stable and the floor was clear of debris.

"Careful," he cautioned Peter as they stepped through the entrance. "Don't rush ahead."

"Cooee," Dr Webb's voice bounced and echoed down the passageway. No lights glowed and the passage disappeared into darkness. "Just as well we brought torches," Dr Webb said as he stepped through the doorway and stood, looking around. "Seems fairly solid here. No damage I can see."

"Plenty of damage further on," someone said, and they turned in surprise. A stab of fear pulsed through Mathew as he regarded Fogarty, no longer tied, and standing with hands on hips, glaring at them. He was a big man. "Did you forget something and you've come back to fetch it?" Sarcasm laced his tone.

"Ah, Mr Fogarty, so glad you are free. We were concerned you'd still be tied up," said Dr Webb.

"I was really worried about you," added Peter, "and I said you'd be cross."

"Lots more to worry about than being cross, Peter." Fogarty stepped forward and ruffled Peter's hair. "You did me a favour in the end. Your parents came looking for you when you didn't go home from your shift. They untied me."

"So they know I went outside?" Fogarty nodded. "Did they mind? Are they alright? Do you know?" The teenager's voice broke and he wiped his eyes and face with his sleeve.

"So many questions. Just give me a minute to explain." He held Peter's gaze. "Your parents were naturally upset but realised you'd grabbed the opportunity to have an adventure. At least, during the earthquake, they would have known you were safe outside. Remember that, because we don't know where they are now." He nodded to Mathew and Dr Webb. "Thank you for returning. I guess you are here to see who survived?"

"We are, and to help them," said Mathew. "I couldn't let Dr Webb come alone, and Peter volunteered to return." He smiled at the young man. "We were shaken off our feet with the quake yesterday morning and watched in horror as the mountain rolled and bucked. It must have been terrifying here, so close. It was bad enough seeing huge slabs of rock slide down the mountainside."

Fogarty rubbed his chin. "Wasn't very nice. The noise was the worst. It was like the mountain was screaming in pain." He took a deep breath. "Still and all, here I am untouched, so I'm very lucky."

"Have many people been hurt? Has anyone come to the exit?" Dr Webb peered into the darkness.

"I've had a look. Haven't just sat around since then, but the passageway is partially blocked and I'm too large to navigate around the rockfall. I tried to move some rocks but they are too large and stuck fast." He considered the rescue party. "You could get by," he said to Peter. "And possibly you, too," he said to Mathew. "But you and I, Dr Webb, are too wide."

The doctor looked crestfallen and chewed his lip. Mathew patted his arm. "Don't worry Doc, we'll go looking, won't we, Peter?"

"Yes, I can get through narrow places. I'm a bit thin."

"We'll see who's alive and we'll get as much of your medicine as we can, Dr Webb."

"You can stay here with me until they return, Doc." Fogarty said, "And tell me about the great outdoors, 'cause I guess I'll be looking for another job. There's no future standing here anymore with no goods coming in and no one trying to get out."

Mathew patted the coil of rope at his waist. "Do you think we'll need this? Along with the backpacks, we don't want to carry anything extra if we don't have to."

"No idea," said Fogarty, "But I'd take it. You don't know how the rockfaces have moved down there. There hasn't been any further noise overnight, except for the odd creak and crack, but if another quake comes you might need it to get out." He paused and snapped his fingers. "I have a map of the passages in the office. I'll get it." He disappeared through a small doorway and returned moments later with a roll of paper and two torches. "Here, I'll swap these for a drink of water, if you have any."

Dr Webb handed him a water bottle. "Have some of mine, seeing as I won't be working up a thirst."

"Thank you." Fogarty gulped some of the water before explaining, "The torches are solar-powered and fully charged. At least the solar panels and batteries are still functioning. I charged them so I could search until I came to that rockfall and couldn't go any further. They should last six hours. You will need to be back before then or you will be trapped in the dark."

"We have a couple of torches as well, but we will keep them as reserves." Mathew unrolled the map and stretched it out on the wall while he and Peter studied it. "Do you think you can find your way around?" he asked the boy.

"Yes, I'm used to wandering around the tunnels. Shouldn't even need the map, but we might need to use some of the service tunnels if the main passages are blocked." He pointed to the narrow lines linking some of the tunnels. "I didn't know there were so many."

Mathew rolled the map up and slid it down inside his jacket. He had a drink from his canister and pointed to Peter for the lad to do the same. "We need to hurry on." He extended his hand to Fogarty "Thank you Mr Fogarty, much appreciated."

"Call me Cyril," Fogarty said.

"Then thank you again, Cyril. I'll leave Dr Webb in your care. Hopefully, we can bring some survivors back with us and I'm sure his skills will be needed then." He turned and followed Peter, who was already hurrying into the darkness, backlit by the circle of light from his torch.

"Wait up," he called.

"He won't get far," Cyril said, "the rockfall will stop him shortly." And so it did.

A few minutes' walk into the inky atmosphere their torches lit the pile of rubble. On one side the floor had sunk about a metre, bringing part of the roof down with it. Hard against the other wall was a gap in the rocks, a tight squeeze but with care and by pushing their backpacks in front of them they crawled over, through and around to the other side. The air on this side had an acrid odour, damp and sharp with a copper tang. It reminded Mathew of spilt blood or ozone by the sea. The tunnel entrance had fresh air drifting in. Little had travelled to this side of the obstruction. Peter didn't comment on the smell. Perhaps this is how it always smelt.

"Watch out for hanging exposed wires," he said. "Don't touch them. I have a pair of rubber gloves that Will Jasper loaned me. If there is residue electricity in the lines I'll be able to handle them safely. If you touch them they could kill you. Understand?" Peter nodded. "Good. I know you want to find your parents but we should go to the closest places first, like Dr Webb's office, which is just up from the main dining area, if I remember correctly. Can you take us there?"

"Yes, I know the way. And once we've done that, can we then check the family units?"

"Of course. I need to see if I can find Eleanor, Calista's mother. Perhaps this time she might be brave enough to leave the mountain."

"She can't stay here now. No one can," said Peter, and he pointed ahead at yet another pile of rock, this time fallen from the ceiling. "And look at that." He pointed to a crack in the wall where a thin stream of moisture oozed. Not yet a trickle, but building. "That'll cause flooding somewhere when it gets to the bottom." He reached toward the trickle.

"Don't touch it. It could be contaminated, so don't even think about drinking it." Mathew warned. "We have no idea what tanks have been ruptured in the quake. I would bet everything is now mixed together." He gripped the boy's shoulder. "We may need to be very brave, Peter. Things may not be good further on." He hoped whatever they came across didn't scar the boy for life with memories he couldn't forget. "I'm so glad of your company, and we will do the best to find your parents." Peter sniffed and rubbed his arm across his face. "Right, lead on young man," said Mathew and they moved forward in the dark, skirting the pile of rocks, following the rock-walled passage until the floor of the tunnel dropped in front of them.

"We have come back this way, so we'll leave a short piece of rope tied here. It's too abrupt to climb back up without something to haul on, even if we can leap down now. Hopefully, we'll be carrying supplies on our return. Or injured people," he added, although the utter silence didn't bode well for the likelihood of survivors.

"I'll do it," Peter said and tied one end of his rope length to a metal bracket in the wall that had once held a lamp. They both slid down the drop and took the left-hand turn toward the dining area.

The smell of death, and the acrid tang of stale food close to fermentation, greeted them before they reached the dining area. From the doorway, they could see most of the roof had fallen. Around the edge the legs of tables and chairs protruded, like the legs of squashed beetles. The huge slab now formed the top of a rock sandwich. Nothing could have survived the collapse, and it looked as if it had happened in a split second. He could only hope it had and that the end had been instant for those having their breakfast.

"Anyone there?" Mathew called, hoping no one would answer. What could they do if someone was still alive and trapped? Only the sound of running water broke the ensuing silence.

"Let's move on," he murmured, and nudged Peter gently ahead. "Next stop, the doctor's office."

Devastation greeted them once more. The office had been ransacked. The shelves were stripped, every drawer in the desk had been pulled out and emptied. A lone model skeleton stood in one corner like a spectator to the decimation. "We can't carry that back," said Peter. "I wish we could. It's cool."

"I guess Dr Webb doesn't need it anyway," said Mathew. "He must know all the bones in the body, but he might like these." He pointed to the posters and charts on the wall, depicting the body's muscles and various organs. Mathew carefully removed them and rolled them up, again putting them inside his jacket.

In the litter on the floor, Peter found and assembled the model of a heart and under a surgical trolley they found some bottles of medicine and rolls of bandages, overlooked by the looters.

"This proves that people survived," said Mathew, "That's a positive thing. They would have needed to take everything of use with them. They may have found the broken floor too high to climb without ropes and perhaps saw the rockfall. I'd guess they decided to use another exit."

Peter's face brightened "Perhaps Mum and Dad are with them. There're more exits. One to the west and another on the eastern side, called E3."

"There's even the train line that people could have used to escape." That could be blocked as well, but he didn't express his thoughts aloud. Better to give the boy hope.

They wandered around opening every cupboard and looking into corners, picking up anything at all that had been left — a box of safety pins, some packets of surgical needles, more bandages, a box of wooden tongue depressors and down the side of the couch some packets of tablets, which must have fallen there during the hurried gathering by the quake survivors. Everything went into their back packs and with a final look around to make sure they hadn't left anything useful behind they left, hurrying past the silent dining area and on toward the living quarters.

Three times the passages were blocked and each time they checked the map and took a service tunnel to get around the obstacle. The tunnels through the rock had been lifted and dropped, fractured into pieces — even in one place moved sideways, the whole passage blocked by a flat rockface. Twice they had to backtrack and try another way when they'd walked all the way down a service tunnel only to find they couldn't get through the far end. Once, Mathew took his small axe to a doorway to release a lock from its wooden frame. Often he lifted wires out of their way, careful to wear the rubber gloves, not daring to test whether they were alive with electricity. The stench of decay followed them everywhere, the tunnels warmer than he'd expected. Here and there a body lay across their path, with obviously fatal injuries. Twisted torsos, crushed limbs and blood loss had contributed to their deaths. Mathew ushered Peter on and he waited, his gaze averted, while Mathew checked for signs of life. Each corpse slowed their progress and time ticked on.

"I hope you are keeping track of where we're going because I'm now completely lost," Mathew said as they exited the sixth service tunnel. "Prop that door open, Peter, so we know we used it. Surely we must be nearly there."

"I live just down here," Peter called over his shoulder as he raced ahead and Mathew hoped whatever greeted him would be bearable. He'd smelt death on their way here. It permeated every crevice, along with the other odours, especially the smell of the wastewater tanks. He caught up to Peter as the lad stood at the door of his home. Inside, the furniture came into view like a slide show as the torch beam crossed and re-crossed the room. There was no sign of bodies or death, not even in the bedrooms, much to Mathew's relief. "They must have made it out," he said, and watched as Peter scrabbled in a bedside table drawer and tossed a few things into his bag. He removed a crocheted rug from a bed and stuffed it into his backpack. "My granny made me this," he said, a catch in his voice. "She died last year."

"Right, time to move on then," Mathew said. "Now to look for Eleanor."

It was a horrible thing to think but life would be less complicated if she'd died. The thought of Eleanor meeting Aaron's common-law wife Angela didn't evoke a pleasant picture. Once married to Calista, Mathew would have a father-in-law and two mothers-in-law., all of whom might be embroiled in domestic war. Not easy for Calista, either. She had yet to face her father with her knowledge of his second family.

His worrying halted with Peter saying, "Here we are, the Waterman's residence."

It looked as if nothing had been touched. If Eleanor had left, she'd done so in a rush to safety. The spinning wheel stood in a corner and he knew Calista would love to have it, but he couldn't take it. Instead he reached high and retrieved all the skeins of wool he could squash into a nearby drawstring bag. They weighed little and packed down tight. He looked around wondering what else she would like him to get. Whatever he took needed to be unbreakable. From the dresser drawer, he took a set of six silver spoons, several yellowed, bone-handled knives that must be very old, and a small silver jug. The latter needed a good clean but it must be a treasure. He remembered seeing one like it once. Beside Eleanor's bed, he found a rosary with amber beads, another ancient treasure. He slipped all of them in with the wool. He took one last look around, knowing there must be things he'd missed and should take. He'd never be back and possibly no one else would either. The whole complex would become a common grave. Sadness overwhelmed him as reality hit and he drew a ragged breath. Enough. They had to get back.

He checked his watch. Just over five hours had passed and they needed to hurry. Even so, they'd be using the back-up torches by the time they climbed the last rock shelf. At least now they wouldn't be back-tracking. They had a clear route to follow. They couldn't afford to get lost and be stranded in the dark.

"Come on, Peter. Time to go. You lead the way."

The lad picked up two soft toys from the floor and stuffed them into the top of the wool bag. "For Vanily and Caleb," he murmured and then hurried ahead.

Never had a rope looked so good. By the time they reach the last ledge, where it dangled, they were exhausted. Their drink bottles were empty and their torch beams fading. Once on top of the ledge they retrieved the rope and trudged on to where they had to squeeze through the final gap.

"Nearly home," he called as loud as he could manage, and heard a faint reply, "Coming to the rockfall." It sounded like Cyril's voice. Willing hands reached through the gap and pulled their backpacks through ahead of them, and then the bag of wool and trinkets. Finally Peter wriggled over and through, and then Mathew followed, glad to be out of the dank tunnels. He inhaled great breaths. His lungs appreciated the ice-laden air. It smelt of snow and rain, of trees and clothes dried in the wind. He swore the air even smelled of sunshine. He took deep breaths, leaving Peter to tell of their search and the maze of tunnels they'd explored.

"No survivors?" Dr Webb asked in a quiet aside, his eyebrows high.

"Yes, some people survived and cleaned out your clinic, which is good news in one respect and bad news in another, but we took anything that was left. At least there were some who survived, but"—he took a deep breath—"many didn't. That much was obvious." He refused to say anymore.

Chapter 4

Mathew thought going down the mountain would be easy, but it became a jarring event, as they slid on haunches and heels, needing to stop and regroup every little while. They each veered off in a different direction on the gravel scree. Sharp rocks protruded, their edges reaching to cut them, and even the smooth edges of boulder bruised their legs. Filthy, their mouths full of dust, their eyes gritty and their bones aching, they finally reached a dirt platform above the flat plain, but not as close as to where their climb had begun early that morning.

"Damn, now we'll have to walk about half a mile," Mathew said, brushing his trousers free of debris and rubbing his aching back. "Surely they must have seen us sliding down. We created enough dust."

"Not to mention noise," Dr Webb added with a smile, because Cyril Fogarty and Peter Tonkin had whooped and yahooed frequently during their rapid descent. They'd acted like youngsters released from a forced and boring confinement. "Perhaps they wondered where we would land."

"I didn't know myself," Mathew agreed. "Oh well, more walking it is, so let's begin. Can't be that far along." He hobbled for a few steps before he got into a rhythm, but his strides were shorter than usual as they descended the rolling mounds which stretched in a gentle slope down to the plain below. It had been a long, strenuous day and his body reminded him of it with every step.

From higher up they'd spied the wagons, tiny dark blocks on the beige plain. The horses would be grazing nearby or resting under the shade of the sparsely scattered trees. No sign of the tent.

With luck it would be up before they reached the wagons and their companions would have hot tea and some food waiting. A brief lie-down in the shade of a tree seemed like a blissful dream as he put one foot in front of the other. Never had he felt so tired.

He turned and checked on Dr Webb, who was striding along beside him. Peter and Cyril also seemed in good spirits, but then Peter had youth on his side and to Cyril this was the beginning of a new life. After two days of standing at the E5 exit, Mathew guessed any sort of exercise would be welcome to the ex-guard, whose personality had blossomed over the hours. He'd turned out to be a really great fellow, strong, willing and cheerful. He'd insisted on wearing one of the backpacks and carrying the other slung over his shoulder on their descent down the mountain. Dr Webb had the bag of wool and bits and pieces so at least Mathew and Peter were free of any weight after their six hours of searching through the Erewhon community tunnels.

They rounded a small spur jutting out into the plain and stopped in astonishment. A large group of people were gathered around the wagons, some standing, some grouped on the ground, others lying in the shade of the trees. Several children ran among the adults, their high-pitched voices carried on the wind and a baby cried in sudden distress. Survivors, a dozen or more, not counting the children. And where were Castor's men? As they approached Mathew scanned the crowd, a sense of unease creeping through his veins. Then he spied them: Alvin by the horses, Kieran and Jonothan each standing on a wagon, their stance rigid and alert. Guarding the horses? Guarding the wagons?

On seeing them, Kieran jumped down from the wagon and walked toward them, his arm raised in greeting, "Great to see you back," he called. "Only one extra? No other survivors?"

Mathew shook his head. When Keiran reached him he added, "No. We searched for five hours in as many tunnels as we could. Saw quite a few bodies and evidence of many crushed." He shook Kieran's hand and nodded to the gathered crowd. "Looks like you have company. Survivors?"

"Yes, they arrived about midday. I've given them most of the food and water, but have kept some for you."

"Thank heavens for that. I'm starving," Peter said.

The five of them stopped and looked at the wagons and the

collection of people. "They say they escaped through something called Exit E3 late yesterday afternoon," Kieran said, "and then made their way down the range, but stopped on a plateau overnight."

"That would be right. I know that exit," Cyril said.

Kieran beckoned them to keep walking toward the wagons. "We need to hurry, things are tense. They saw us this morning from their lookout and headed this way."

"Any injuries?" Dr Webb asked, "I can hear a baby crying."

"She's probably hungry," Kieran said. "We've given her water but she wants milk. There're two young women with four children from the crèche. They grabbed the kids and ran when the quake began to collapse their rooms. The poor children are probably orphans now. But it's still a big adventure to them. They can't believe the space to run in."

"Are we staying the night? Perhaps we should put the tent up," Mathew said.

"Honestly, I'd rather not. There're a couple of wide-boys in the group. I don't like the look of them and I trust them even less. I've noticed men gathering in groups of two or three, with intense conversations going on." He pointed to the horses. "I've got young Alvin guarding them, keeping them together."

He stopped and clapped Mathew on the shoulder "So glad you're back."

"Meet Cyril Fogarty," Mathew said, extending his arm in Cyril's direction. "Cyril, this is Kieran, one of the foremen from Castor Seville's farm."

The men shook hands, and Kieran ran his gaze up and down the newcomer. "We might need your size if push comes to shove." He grinned. "Nice uniform."

Cyril raised his chin and scoffed. "Looks totally ridiculous in the daylight; I'll be glad to find some other clothes."

Moments later they'd reached the edge of the group and Kieran led them through the crowd. Mathew shook his head when queried by the people he passed "Sorry. No, we looked everywhere. No, didn't check the train station or lines, only the accommodation area."

At Kieran's instruction he stopped at the end of the wagon and hauled himself up to sit on the edge. Immediately, he could feel the tension in the air. Kieran's assumption was correct; something or someone had stirred these people up.

"Could you say a few words?" Kieran said in a quiet aside.

He nodded, but turned and looked for his bo, his Kempo fighting stick. There it was, tucked along the side of the wagon, hard and polished. He reached and dragged it close, feeling better knowing he had some protection from the suppressed emotions simmering in this crowd.

"Welcome everyone," he said. "So great you've made it this far. I'm sorry, I can't tell you of any other survivors but we looked and did our best. We found bodies, but no one alive. You escaped, obviously, and maybe there are others, but we didn't come across anyone else." He took a deep breath, knowing the next news would hurt "We stopped by the dining room and I'm sorry to say that anyone at breakfast when the quake struck would now be dead. The roof had collapsed and there was no sign of life in that area." One of the men moaned and had to be supported by the person next to him. "Kieran tells me he's given you food and water, as much as we can spare. If we hurry back this afternoon we can reach safe accommodation by evening, although it will be dark by the time we get there."

"And where's that going to be?" The query had a snarl in it from a man near the front of the gathering.

"It's a farm about five to six hours' walk, but it will be faster with the wagons. Some of you must walk and take turns riding. Pregnant women and children can ride of course, but we only have the two wagons"

"And spare horses." This time a slightly built man moved to the front and stood beside the tall fellow who'd queried a moment before.

"True, but they are taken. Peter and I have spent most of the day in the tunnels, and we shall be using two of them." He didn't even know if Peter could ride a horse, but at least he could sit on one and save his legs.

He carried on. "Once there you can decide what you want to do. You might like to work on the farm for Mr Seville, or you might decide to go on to Quake City and start a life there." He raised his voice above the murmuring. "You are free to do what you want. No one is going to tell you how to live your life in the future, but I think your priority, just now, is to find shelter and food before you make any decisions."

The man who had snarled stepped closer. Mathew could smell tobacco on him. Even with Mathew sitting on the back of the wagon, his eyes were level with man's. He was a big man, wide and tall with it. "And what if I need a horse and I want to go south? What are you going to do about that, sonny? I want to know who put you in charge."

It was a challenge, laced with menace, followed by murmurs in the crowd. A threat he couldn't ignore. This is what Kieran had been feeling earlier.

"I did," shouted Dr Webb. "I'm your doctor and I put him in charge of searching for survivors. He's been magnificent."

The bully turned and swung his elbow in an arc, hitting the doctor in the chest. "Oh shut up, little man," he hissed. This action gave Mathew the time he needed and the excuse to act.

He grabbed his bo, slid off the wagon's end and by the time the bully turned back Mathew had his stick held chest high, his hands spread wide on its length. He stepped forward and pushed hard against the bully's chest, marching him backward several paces and almost toppling him over. The crowd retreated, making space. He could feel Cyril's presence at his side, could hear his breathing, ready to assist, but at that moment Mathew had the advantage. The bully stumbled and as he regained his balance he pulled a gun from under his shirt.

It might not be loaded. Bullets were a scarce commodity but Mathew wasn't taking any chances. With an upward swing he hit the bully's wrist, knocking the gun out of his hand. As it hit the ground Cyril kicked it away and Mathew stood ready, waiting for the bully's next move, knowing the doctor or one of Kieran's men would have picked the gun up.

"You little bastard," the man cursed. "No one beats me in a fight." He clasped his wrist. Pain etched his face. "You've broken it." His voice was shrill with pain.

"I might have," said Mathew, "but it's bad manners to pull a gun on someone."

"What about a knife then?" The thin man had stepped up beside the bully, his knife clenched at waist-height, ready to stab or slice. Mathew switched his grip on the bo, turned side on and swung his weapon in a horizontal arc aiming for the man's chest. It connected with a loud thud. The communal gasp meant many heard the crack as it hit the man's ribs. The small man buckled over in pain, his knife dropping to the ground. As the bully moved in to pick it up with his remaining good hand, Mathew kicked out high and fast, connecting with the bully's shoulder. This time the man hit the dirt, winded and silent.

"Tie him up," Mathew yelled, confident Cyril would cope and turned again to the smaller of the two. "Do you want to continue?"

The small man shook his head. "He said he'd get us a couple of horses. I wouldn't normally hurt anyone."

"Too late to say that now." Mathew nodded to Cyril. "Tie him up, too,"

He stood, breathing deeply, calming the surplus energy racing around his body, trying to remember Winston's lessons about only causing damage if you really had to—preventing violence, not indulging in it—and otherwise words that at this moment he couldn't recall.

A firm hand clasped his shoulder. "Well done, young man. That was brave." Cyril's voice, quiet in his ear.

"Or totally foolish." The red mist began to fade from his brain and his thoughts cleared.

Kieran climbed onto the wagon and addressed the crowd. "Anyone else think they can take a horse?" Only the sound of feet scuffing the hard dirt broke the silence. "We don't care if you want to go south." Kieran pointed to the end of the Southern Alps. "It's a long walk, but you'll find Lake Tekapo, then take the inland route to Twizel, and on to Wanaka and Queenstown. You might even find other survivors on your way. I wish you luck, but the rest of us are now going to head home to the farm. You can come or you can stay."

Cyril climbed and stood beside him. "I've decided to go on to the farm. Like all of you I no longer have a home or a job," he said, brushing his uniform, "and until I get some other clothes I'm stuck wearing this silly outfit." There were a few chuckles from the crowd. "I didn't have family in the tunnels and I'm so sorry for those of you who did but remember some may have escaped down the train tunnel. Who knows how many went south that way. There's always hope, but from this moment on I'm going to start a new life. I might be big and scary in my uniform"—more laughter—"but I'm as frightened as any of you of what lies ahead."

A ragged cheer erupted from the gathering. The children, having watched the proceedings as if it were for their entertainment, began another game of chasey. The baby began to cry again and one of the women began to weep. Mathew turned his back on the noise and watched Alvin bring the horses back and Jonothan begin to guide people up onto the wagons.

"Did you find any bullets?" Mathew said when Cyril approached him.

"Four in his pocket, and one in the gun. I have them, and the gun is no longer loaded."

His chest tightened. The gun had been loaded, he could have been shot. "Could you look after it, keep it in a safe place? They might make a break for it."

"I wouldn't be sad to see them go. Do we need to look after them? We could actually abandon them on the way or leave them here."

Mathew looked over at the two men, hands trussed and sitting back to back, pictures of dejection. "I'm a Carbonite," he said, "and we don't believe in violence or punishment. I shouldn't have hurt them so badly. I lost my temper."

"I'd probably have done worse if I had your skill." Cyril ran his hand over his head and dust rose in a fine cloud, burnished by the afternoon sun.

"I think we have to take them to Seville's and let Will Jasper decide what to do with them," Mathew said. "He must have experience with malfeasants, more experience than we have." When Cyril didn't say anything Mathew continued thinking aloud. "Guns are illegal outside of the tunnels. The authorities have them, but it's the bullets they keep under lock and key. Without bullets a gun is pretty useless. You can only use it as you would any small object, like throwing it at someone."

Exhaustion hit him like a strong wind and he folded to sit on the ground, his bo across his lap, gazing at the mountain range that was causing so much pain and suffering to people. He heard Cyril's footsteps recede then the sound of another person approaching.

"Thank you, Mathew." He looked up to Dr Webb's round face. "You've done miracles today. I'm so proud to know you." A water bottle wavered into his view. "Here, have a drink then I recommend you climb up beside Kieran and watch the scenery as we head back to Seville's farm. I'm going to check everyone while we travel, but

35

they look okay. They've made it this far with only a few scrapes and bruises. The only major injuries are those you inflicted, but they were deserved."

Mathew winced at the sound of the baby's thin wail.

"I know" the Doctor said. "It's heart-breaking to listen to. I'll give her some water and hope she will suck on a piece of apple. She's only a few months old. Once we're at the farm I'll get milk for her There might even be someone there who could breastfeed her."

"Yes," Mathew murmured as he climbed to his feet, his legs again stiff and sore. Chance would be a fine thing—he couldn't imagine anyone having spare breast milk, but the farm had plenty of cows' milk. "Babies are our future. We need to look after her."

"Don't worry, I will, even if I have to rock her to sleep myself," Dr Webb said.

The doctor, Mathew then realised, was another survivor of the tunnels. He may have walked out before the quake, following Calista, but the community had been the doctor's family. He too must be feeling great sorrow at the huge loss of life among his patients, and his inability to save anyone. All the more reason for the Carbonites to build a clinic for him—just as soon as they could get back to the stockade. This band of survivors would give the good doctor a purpose and occupy his time caring for them until they made it back to Quake City.

Chapter 5

The rumble of wagon wheels on the driveway and the sound of familiar voices reached Calista. She moved around the kitchen helping Mrs Rasmussen clean up after preparing for the evening meal, yet another huge pot of stew to meet an unknown number of diners. She could hear Winston's loud voice and then others joining in. She stopped, and tilted her head, trying to recognise whose voice it was shouting in reply.

Her father? Surely not? How could he be here when he was supposed to be in Quake City? She wiped her hands on her apron and hurried outside. There he was, high on the driver's seat of a huge wagon behind a horse she hadn't seen before. A large chestnut with a white blaze and four white socks, it almost blocked her view. Dragging her gaze away from the magnificent animal, she saw behind them a smaller wagon pulled by Bess, the Carbonite's other draught horse. They came to a halt beside the kitchen door, and once Winston had taken the chestnut's bridle, her father jumped down and wrapped her in his arms.

"My darling, precious daughter," he said, kissing her head, cupping her cheeks in his rough hands, his beard tickling her face as he whispered in her ear, "I'm so glad to see you. I'm so happy you're safe. I've missed you and I'm wracked with guilt that no one could help you the night you were kidnapped." She buried her face in his shirt, inhaling his familiar scent and cherishing the sense of security and love his embrace gave her.

"Let me look at you." Aaron held her at arm's length, his gaze running over her. She could see him searching for injury or harm, but having found none his face relaxed and he grinned "You look wonderful, despite your second dash to freedom."

"I'm just fine, thanks to Mathew. Did you know I was here?"

"Yes, we heard about the earthquake and the devastation of the mountain range. The rumbles reached Quake City but were much weaker. Winston used the radiotelephone, here on the farm, to let us know you and the others had made it to safety." Castor Seville had radio contact with Quake City. Another fact to file away for the future. Every day she learned something new. "Have you come to take us all home to the stockade?"

Her father looked away to the horizon, where the snow-capped Alps drew a white line in the late afternoon light. "Yes and no, not exactly." He pointed to the large wagon and new horse. "I've borrowed these and, along with our wagon, we're going to scale the mountainside and retrieve the solar panels and batteries. Remember where we climbed out of that service door into the moonlight?"

She nodded. She'd never forget the starry sky, the moon and the smell of the fresh crisp air.

Aaron continued, "I'll wait until Mathew returns and hear what he has to say, but I believe the Erewhon community won't need them anymore."

She raised her eyebrows and opened her mouth to object. The survivors within the tunnels may have great need of them, her mother included. How could he just take them?

"They are precious, Calista. We can't get them anymore and if the community is destroyed then we must rescue the panels and use them in Quake city for the good of the community."

Always "the community", but then he was the leader of the Carbonites, and like a band of monks, they worked tirelessly for those in need, so she swallowed her objections. They would wait for Mathew to return.

Around them, their fellow Carbonites mingled, moving off with the wagons, unloading produce from the city's gardens. Benjamin walked past carrying a large box of cauliflower and broccoli.

"Mrs Rasmussen will be pleased to see those," she said. "You might even get a kiss," she added, teasing him, remembering the Carbonites enjoyed the fruits of his friendship with Castor Seville's cook.

He turned and blessed her with a grin. "You've got a bit cheeky, Miss Calista, since you left us and went to Cheviot," he said, but he wasn't cross. A slight pink blush that wasn't sunburn rose up his neck.

"And I'm delighted to see you too, Benjamin," she called after him.

Within moments she and her father were standing alone, and the air between them tightened. The conversation she'd dreaded had to begin and she knew the time had arrived. She couldn't speak. The words wouldn't trip off her tongue. They lined up and then disappeared and another phrase lined up. None seemed appropriate. Finally, her father spoke.

"Your mother…"

She nodded and waited.

"Winston told me she didn't come with you."

"No, she was coming with us, all the way to the exit, but at the last moment she passed Vanily to Pelly and just disappeared back down the tunnel." Her voice caught "She didn't even say goodbye, Father. She just left us. By the time I found out it was too late to go back and get her." The memory tugged at her heart, a sharp sense of loss.

"I'm not surprised." He put his arm around her shoulder and hugged her to his side. They both looked again toward the western horizon. "She was born in the tunnels. Never knew anything else. I wanted you both to come with me all those years ago when I first left, and she wouldn't come." The silence grew, and then he added. "I warned her I would return for you, and when I did I guess she was happy for you to leave because she had the two children and felt you would return to them."

"Which I did—reluctantly," Calista said. "I didn't mean for her to be left behind. I'm not sure I'd have left without her."

"She would have known that. It's probably why she went along with the plan, until the last moment. Getting that close to the exit would have terrified her. I believe she suffers from agoraphobia, the fear of open spaces."

"Suffers? You think she may have survived the quakes?"

"We won't know until Mathew returns, but let's hope she will come with him. This time, because of the earthquake, fear may drive her out, rather than keep her in," her father said.

And now the moment had arrived and this time she grasped it. "Won't that be a bit embarrassing for you?"

He took a step back and raised his eyebrows.

"You know quite well what I mean, Father. You have another wife and two children." He looked again at the Alps. She hurried on before her courage failed her. "Betty told me, in Cheviot, just before I left. I said I was your only daughter and she corrected me. I know about Angela—and Belinda and Colin, my two half-siblings." He looked over her shoulder at the house. "I remember the day at the Ferrymead Market and the little blonde girl, who looked so familiar. She called out 'Daddy'. You said she was just a confused child, but she was your daughter and you ignored her." It sounded harsh but it was true. "And the young boy raised his arm to me, in a wave of acknowledgement. He knew who I was." Her voice was getting high, so she stopped speaking. After a while, she added: "It's none of my business really, but I'd like to meet them, and it's your problem to explain to Mother, not mine. I'm certainly not going to tell her." She slipped her arm through his, hugging his elbow. "Come on, come and meet your grandchildren again. It's months since you've seen them."

They walked toward the accommodation block but after a short distance, Aaron pulled her to a halt. "It's the way of the world now, Calista. Women need protection and while your mother never asked me, I'm quite sure she would have assumed I would take a common-law wife outside. I lost my family when she wouldn't come and I fell in love with Angela."

"I decided a while ago that it wasn't my place to judge you, Father. I'm just hurt that you didn't tell me. It seems everyone knew but me. I'm no longer a child. You could have told me."

"It never seemed to be the right time."

"Like you couldn't tell me that Castor Seville was pursuing me in Quake City and perhaps further north?" Her voice quiet and firm, she held his gaze "Mathew tells me Castor has a new wife, which is a relief—but no more secrets, Father, please." Never mind she presently hugged a secret of her own.

"I didn't want to offend Castor. We need his support, but I was determined he wasn't going to have my daughter when I'd just freed you from breeding servitude. By removing you from his influence I hoped to walk the fine line of diplomacy."

They walked on. "Let's hope I did," he continued, "because we need him. For all his faults and his huge ego, Castor allows us the use of his buildings and farm as a staging post."

"And Will Jasper loaned Mathew and Dr Webb horses and men to go and look for survivors,' said Calista. "Some of the people that came with me are already talking about staying here, but I'm hoping some will come to Quake City and help the Carbonites."

"Good girl," her father said, hugging her again. "Now let's go and see my grandchildren."

They were eating dinner in the main house kitchen, spread around the large central table that doubled as a workbench between meals, when Pelly ran into the room, her face alight with excitement.

"They're coming! They're coming! Daphne and I have just seen them. Small shapes on the broken road, heading this way. They'll be here in half an hour, Daphne reckons."

The Carbonites, favoured with these eating arrangements, rather than eating in the communal dining room with the farmworkers and survivors, beamed and nodded at Pelly, most seeing her for the first time.

Calista's heart tightened. She was excited at the thought of seeing Mathew, hoping he was okay and that her mother was with them. And then her enthusiasm sank again at the prospect of the meeting between her mother and father. Why did life have to be so complicated? It wasn't her problem, she reminded herself, and continued to eat her meal, yet another hearty stew, full of vegetables and rich with meat and bone marrow stock. She rose to check the contents of the pot, wondering if there was enough left to feed the arriving wagons.

Mrs Rasmussen stood beside her. "Don't fret, pet, there's more food in the chiller I can heat and all the bread we baked today will no doubt be gone by bedtime. There's plenty of food over in the community kitchen, plus there's always porridge for the morning. God bless oats and wheat." They turned back to the table to finish their meal. Both knew the Carbonites would clear up and do the dishes tonight. No wonder Mrs Rasmussen liked them. Calista noted that Mrs Rasmussen and Benjamin touched hands occasionally when standing close to each other and at this moment were seated side by side. There could be a quiet romance growing there; even if the rest of the Carbonites hadn't noticed it, she had.

An hour later the wagons arrived at the front gates. The horses, knowing they were close to home and their stables, broke into a trot once through the entrance. The wagons rolled up the tree-lined drive, leaving those on foot behind. The walkers, too tired to hurry, straggled in, some barely able to lift their feet. Jason Fletcher and Samuel Hager hurried toward them with shouts of welcome and as a group, the new arrivals straightened their backs and stepped with purpose.

The news had spread and the families and youngsters that had escaped with Calista, mingled with the farmworkers. A buzz of excitement and anticipation stirred the gathering, all hoping for good news and dreading the bad.

Calista swept her gaze over the walking survivors, all men, then searched the wagons for the familiar shape of her mother's head. Nothing. She checked again in case her mother's outline was obscured. No. Unless she was lying on the wagon's deck, she wasn't in the group. Sadness softened her shoulders and she clasped Caleb's hand so tight he grimaced and withdrew it.

"Caleb," she said. "Stand here next to Pelly and Vanily. I want to see Mathew."

She wove her way through the crowd gathered around the first wagon, all assisting in helping people off. A baby wailed as if woken from sleep. There were three small children, clinging to a couple of young women. Their wide eyes and trembling lips displayed their fear of the noise and the grasping hands of the helpers.

She dodged around a couple of men into a space behind the tailgate on the first wagon, intending to cross to the other side of the rear wagon, to where Mathew stood talking. Her way forward abruptly became blocked by a group dragging two men off the wagon. Their hands were tied behind their back and as they gained their feet and turned toward her, panic rose in her throat like a sharp stone, the pain making her gasp.

"Well I'll be damned, if it isn't the runaway prime breeder, Miss Calista Waterman," the tall one said, giving her a mock bow. "I see you've escaped once more. I'm glad we got paid for bringing you home the first time." He sneered. "Is there a price on your head this time?"

She couldn't answer and didn't want to. In a rush she pushed past, stepping around the smaller of the two captives, avoiding his gaze and ignoring the shouts and shoving of the men who seemed to be in charge of moving the captives.

In her headlong flight, she tripped and fell against Mathew, grabbing his arm as she stumbled.

"Callie, darling, what's wrong?" He supported her, smoothing her hair, and stroked her cheek. "Are you alright?" Concern softened his face as she held his gaze.

"Those men, the ones with their hands tied up. I know them," she said.

"You do? Good, who are they?" He didn't seem to notice her inability to speak and carried on "The rest of the survivors don't know who they are, except they did help a lot of people escape. But once outside we're told they became very aggressive, demanding money or goods to shepherd the people down the mountain."

Finally the words came: "They're the same two men who kidnapped me. The ones Wallace Howe paid to find me and bring me back to the tunnels."

"What are their names? They won't say."

She shook her head. "They never once uttered each other's name in my hearing. I just thought of them as the big one and the smaller one." She looked back to where a small group were escorting the two away from the wagons. "They never actually hurt me, but they threatened to plenty of times on the journey to Arthur's Pass unless I behaved. Once we reached Erewhon Station they unbound my hands and let me go, saying they'd fulfilled their part of the contract." The memory brought tears to her eyes. "Of course, I ran home to mother and the children, dashed through the dim tunnels, hating that I was back, trapped again. I didn't see them again…until now."

Mathew hugged her close. "Don't worry, they can't take you away again. I think they'll be locked up until Will Jasper decides what to do with them."

"Why are they tied up?"

"They were stirring the people up, wanting to take the horses, even a wagon, and ride south to Wanaka. Then the tall one hit Dr Webb and decided to have a swing at me."

"You had a fight?" She stepped back and searched for any sign of injury, but his face was unmarked except for weary lines filled with dust around his eyes. On a closer examination, she saw that threads hung and small rips were visible, scattered about on his clothes.

"You're all snagged and torn, Mathew. What on earth happened?" and she moved back into his arms.

"A dreadful, long day, with no success, I'm afraid. The only survivors came out of Exit E3 further along the mountain." He kissed the top of her head "I didn't find Eleanor. I'm sorry. The apartment was empty, but I brought back some mementos for you. Things I could carry." He released her and reached onto the wagon's deck. "Here, these are for you. Plus Peter picked up a soft toy each for the children. I shoved them on top." She recognised the drawstring bag he passed her. A relic of her childhood. Something she had once kept her treasures in, but now it was soft and spongy to hug. She pressed her face into the side of the bag, inhaling the smell of clean wool.

"I wanted to bring Eleanor's spinning wheel, but simply couldn't," Mathew said.

"Of course you couldn't. I understand." The prickling behind her eyes warned her of tears, which overflowed and trickled down her cheeks. "You are such a good man. I don't deserve you." She wiped her arm across her face.

"Nonsense, of course you do." He lifted her, the bag squashed between them, and swung her around. "Let's go and give the kids their toys."

They began to walk through the thinning crowd. In the distance she noticed Dr Webb hurrying along with Will Jasper toward one of the family huts. Did Dr Webb have a baby over his shoulder? A thin cry reached them. "Is there a baby?"

"Yes, a very hungry baby. Dr Webb seems to have adopted her at the moment. He'll be looking for someone to breastfeed her. She and three toddlers were so lucky. Their caregivers at the crèche grabbed them and ran when the walls began to fall." He stared in the direction of the mountain range, now hidden in the inky night. "I would imagine she and the others are now orphans."

The enormity of lives lost began to sink in. "How many survivors?" Her mind refused to picture her mother's demise.

"Probably twenty-five, counting your two reprobates."

"What on earth will they all do?" She couldn't get her head around the tally, plus the two families and handful of teenagers that she had convinced to leave before the quake hit. It could have been them.

"They'll either stay here and work for Castor—he always needs workers—or they'll come on to Quake City. All the men will have useful skills, and some have wives and children buried in the rubble. They're shattered, but the city's community will find a use for them and help them heal. At least they're free, even if at the moment they are grieving." His voice hitched and he sighed.

He sounded so tired. Calista wrapped her arm around his waist, leaned into his side, and together they made their way to the accommodation block, where Pelly waited with the children.

She couldn't help thinking, with some guilt, that Mathew not being able to find her mother had removed one awkward meeting from the present chaos they found themselves in. It seemed her father had avoided having to explain his dalliance, yet again.

Chapter 6

The warmth of the room and a full stomach combined to have Calista fighting to keep her eyes open. This was the first meeting of the Carbonites she'd sat in on. Up to now, she'd always been somewhere else, or busy helping Mary Sutton in the kitchen at the stockade. But tonight she sat alongside Mathew around the large table in the farm's main kitchen, in the Big House. Not the kitchen used by the workers, where presently the survivors mingled with the farm workers, hopefully exchanging experiences and making decisions about their future.

This meeting also dwelt on the future—more especially on removing the solar panels from the side of the mountain, between the two main exits. There wasn't a formed track to it, broken or otherwise; in fact, the whole affair seemed to her to be extremely dangerous and foolhardy. She remembered the huge panels reflecting the moonlight on her first night of freedom. She mentally pictured these men climbing the mountainside where no path existed, unbolting the panels and sliding them down the rock face. What if a rope frayed and broke? What if someone lost their footing? She shuddered, thinking of what could go wrong. At least Mathew wouldn't be going. He'd just returned from the cursed Alps, which still displayed a dusting of snow on the highest peaks. It would be cold up there, and the solar panels weren't that far below the white ridges which etched the western horizon like knuckles on a closed fist. The men's voices rumbled back and forth and her mind wandered.

She couldn't contribute anything constructive to the discussion, and her gaze followed Dr Webb, who entered the kitchen with soft steps. Was that the baby he had in a sling across his chest? He saw her, raised his chin in a silent greeting, and beckoned. She rose and joined him by the stove. It was warmer here closer to the fire, and the doctor stood holding his hands over the hob and rubbing them together before he turned his back to the heat.

"Could you please boil some water for me — and scald some milk? Mrs Rasmussen said I can have some milk for the baby. She'll need it tomorrow."

Calista pulled the sling wide with one finger and peeped in. The baby slept, her tiny, perfect eyelids fluttering as she dreamed.

"It looks like she's been fed. The last time I saw you she was crying, propped on your shoulder."

"Yes," he beamed. "Jasper knew one of the workers whose wife had plenty of milk, and she agreed to breastfeed her. It's going to be hard. She's only three months old and I'm going to have to wean her onto cow's milk over the next few days. The lady has agreed to give her the occasional feed, but of course, her child comes first." He bent his head and looked at the peaceful babe exhausted from hours of wailing for food: the water they'd given her was an unnourishing substitute for breastmilk .The doctor's face softened with pleasure and pride. His finger stroked her fine blond hair.

"What are you going to do with her?" A small, orphaned baby could be a major problem for the group.

"I'm going to keep her." Dr Webb, his tone still gentle but with an edge that suggested he'd allow no harm to come to her. "From what Mathew and Peter saw, we can presume she's an orphan. If her mother turns up in the years to come she will be returned to her, but until then I will treat her as my daughter."

"What a wonderful idea," she said, and reached awkwardly over the baby to hug him.

"I think I'll just sit down over there," he said, pointing to an easy chair tucked into the corner nearest the coal range, no doubt a spot that Mrs Rasmussen occupied in quiet moments.

"You go and sit down and I'll sort the baby's milk." She turned back "Do you know her name?"

As he settled back in the chair, the infant resting on his chest, he placed his arm beneath her bottom to support her and replied. "The nursery girls said her mother called her *Daisy*. I think that will do nicely."

"Any father?"

Dr Webb shook his head. "She was a breeder. This is her first child." He held Calista's gaze when he added, "No doubt the community leaders know who her father is, but we can presume those records no longer exist."

She thought of Wallace Howe, the sperm donor of her two children. Hopefully, he no longer existed either.

"And even if we knew her father, and he were alive, would he want her? In amongst this disaster? I doubt it." And with that, he closed his eyes and Calista reckoned he was asleep in moments.

Fifteen minutes later she had two large jugs filled, one with boiled water and one with scalded milk, which she took into the chiller. She left a scribbled note for the doctor tacked to the mantle above the stove. The meeting closed and the men began to stand. She hurried around, her finger to her lips, pointing to Dr Webb, and they all crept out of the room, closing the door behind them.

"I'm going with Aaron to see if we have a solar engineer amongst the survivors. Fingers crossed," Mathew said, and he kissed her gently. "I'll be a while. You go on, I'll come to bed when I've finished."

Later, his cold limbs roused her from a light sleep and she guessed a couple of hours had passed. He wrapped her in a hug and whispered, "All sorted. We leave in the morning."

She woke up fully. "We?" she said. "You're not going, Mathew. Tell me you're not going back, please."

His arms tightened. She turned within his embrace to face him. "I need you here. Castor is due back any day. You know he terrifies me. Please don't go."

"I have to go. I'm a Carbonite. This is what we do. We have to get the panels and batteries. They will be a great advantage at the stockade and to the work we do. We will need the extra energy to power Dr Webb's clinic. Your father thinks building it next door to the stockade is a wonderful idea. I didn't even have to convince him."

"But..." How could he do this? How could he go away when he'd just returned? Fear churned her stomach and she swallowed back tears. "You could be gone for days."

His breath tickled her ear, "Probably will. I've spoken to Cyril Fogarty, the guard from the entrance. Remember him? He's a superb fellow. He's promised to protect you. I've given him my pendant so if you press yours, he'll come immediately." Her fear shrank to a small dot in her mind. Perhaps it would be okay. "Also," Mathew continued, "don't tell a soul, but he has a gun and a few bullets. He won't be afraid to use it if trouble erupts. I'd never leave you unprotected." He kissed her. His warm lips covered hers and his love made her feel safe once more.

When their kiss ended she asked, "Did you find a solar engineer?"

"We did. We have two men who know how to disconnect and reassemble the parts. They've promised to help remove the panels and to come to Quake City and install them. Such good luck after such a ghastly disaster." He sighed, a huge deep breath of sadness.

In the following moments, she listened to his breathing change and regulate as he fell asleep. He hadn't talked about his day in the tunnels. When she asked he just shook his head and murmured 'you don't want to know' and truly, she didn't. Tomorrow, she'd hunt out Peter Tonkin and spend some time with him. If Mathew wouldn't discuss what he'd seen, then Peter must need some emotional support. His parents were missing and no doubt his imagination would picture them killed in many horrid ways. No longer an enthusiastic teenager, today he'd moved among the other youngsters with an air of quiet maturity and she didn't think a bit of mothering would go amiss.

Knowing Mathew and her father could be away for several days, Calista agreed to Cyril's suggestion that he take her on a guided tour of the flour mill, the water wheel that drove it and other sites of interest around their host's expansive property. It filled in the morning and as they arrived back at the shared accommodation she noticed the tension in the air and increased activity all around.

Workers were tidying the grounds, raking paths, trimming the new growth off hedgerows and the whole area looked as if it were vying for a place in a *Homes and Garden* magazine. Not that they had those sort of magazines any longer, but she'd read them on the worldwide web.

"Thank you so much for the guided tour, Cyril." She pointed at the busy workers. "What's the reason for all this? Do you know?"

"I've heard the squire is returning shortly. I guess it's all for him—and his new wife."

"Of course, that'll be it." How could she have forgotten?

"With his return imminent, don't forget I have Mathew's

pendant. Call me at any time you feel unsafe. I have work nearby for Will Jasper. I'm repairing machinery and will be close to the living quarters most of the time." His smile and sensible manner gave her confidence.

After more thanks and a quick goodbye, she headed inside. The urge to sleep, though not as strong as early in her pregnancy, now called her for an afternoon nap. An hour should do and then she'd go to the main house to help Mrs Rasmussen. Spring flowers graced the communal dining tables and the smell of lamb roasting brought saliva to her mouth. Would she ever tire of that particular aroma? She doubted it. Meat had been a rare luxury at Erewhon. She wondered if this pregnancy had made her into a carnivore.

The children were in school, enjoying the educational games Mrs Grayson organised each day. Would she and April be coming to Quake City? Calista hoped so, but if Will Jasper offered her better terms then Mrs Grayson might stay on. There were about a dozen children in total on the farm, all of whom were benefitting from her teaching skills. Plus it stopped them from roaming, annoying the workers and getting in harm's way.

He found her, alone in the kitchen. His large hand descended on her shoulder and she turned in fright. For a big man, he could move silently. She gasped, her heart seeming to fall to her stomach before rebounding and thumping as if to leap out of her chest.

"Mr Saville, you frightened me."

"Please call me *Squire*, Calista. I've been looking for your over at the accommodation block." He clasped her shoulders and held her at arm's length. "Let me look at you." His gaze raked her and a smile curled his lips. "Still as beautiful as ever—if not more so. I hear you've been a busy girl since last we met. Going on holiday north of Quake City, absconding into the bush with a doctor, only to be kidnapped and returned to the tunnels." What could she say? It was true, so she said nothing. "And now you're free once more."

She shrugged from under his grasp and stepped away, busying herself with the cutlery on the table. He didn't move. His gaze again roamed over her. Her skin itched and chilled as if her clothes had been removed.

"How is your wife?" she asked, to distract him.

"She's just wonderful. We arrived a short time ago and she's resting. Bit of a tummy problem she tells me. I'd like you to meet her because my offer to you still stands. I'd like you to be my wife as well. You two could be good friends." She searched for a suitable, polite rejoinder, but he continued as her mind searched for the right words. "Of course you wouldn't be head wife, that would be Josephine, but I can offer you full charge of all activities outside the manor house." Damn the man, had he no shame? "I can see you are not impressed, Miss Waterman, being offered second running. Having more than one wife is common practice these days, even if it's not exactly legal." She knew that from her father's actions. "But who cares about legality when wealth and healthy living is being offered as a reward? What do you say? Can I tempt you?"

This time she had to reply. "No thank you, Squire. I have a partner and we are going to live in Quake City with my father. My partner is a Carbonite." That should stop this ridiculous conversation.

"Perhaps you need to get to know me better?" He stepped quickly and wrapped her in his arms. Her hand flew to her pendant. His mouth pressed against hers, his breath stale, the exertion of his journey still fresh on his body. Her thumb drummed the button on the back of her pendant in a frantic tattoo.

Her body froze as his hands began to search for an opening in her bodice and, not finding one, began to squeeze her buttocks. She wanted to bite his lips but remembered how the Carbonites depended on this man's generosity for their work. She struggled within his embrace, breaking his kiss, writhing and imploring, "Stop, Squire, leave me alone or I'm going to scream, loudly." His grip didn't ease.

A door slammed against the wall and heavy footsteps approached before a loud cough, and a man said, "Excuse me." Cyril had come after all.

"Excuse me, Squire, sorry to interrupt but Dr Webb is asking for Calista. There's been an accident in the field and she is needed to help him." Seemingly in no hurry to release her, Castor straightened and peered over her shoulder to appraise the man who had interrupted his pleasure. Calista slipped from his grasp to watch the two men. They stood, the same height, eyes level, and Calista could see the squire sizing up his chances with this stranger.

"And who are you?" His nose tilted as if he had smelt a bad odour, but Cyril didn't even blink. He held out his hand and smiled broadly. "I'm Cyril Fogarty, former guard of Exit E5 of the Erewhon

Community and newly recruited Carbonite. Pleased to meet you, sir." It was the 'sir' that softened Castor's stance. Calista could see it written on his face that he assumed this man was another subservient worker he could boss around.

"Damned nuisance, your interruption. I was inviting Miss Waterman to spend her future here with me, in luxury."

"Her partner might object to that...*sir*." Again, Cyril's smile spread wide. It would be hard to pick a fight with a man who was being so charming. Calista hid her smile.

"I could compensate him for his loss," Castor offered.

Now he was trying to buy her! She held her jaws together, swallowing the rising objection.

"Nothing to do with me, Squire. You'd have to ask him personally." Cyril looked at Calista. "There's some urgency to the doctor's request."

"I'll just grab my cape and be with you." She hurried into the foyer, pulled her cape around her shoulders and stood at the kitchen door, waiting while Cyril and Castor finished their polite conversation about the state of the fields, the prospect of more earthquakes and whether Cyril was sure he wanted to travel on to Quake City when there were opportunities for men of his size and strength right here on the farm. Once convinced of Cyril's determination, Castor Seville nodded and stalked out, heading into the manor's living quarters.

Calista grasped Cyril's hand, gratitude bringing tears to her eyes. "Thank you for coming."

"Not a problem. I could see where it was heading," he said, "and it didn't look as if you were enjoying yourself."

She followed him down the steps and along the path. "That's an understatement. My next move would have been to stamp on his foot or knee him, neither of which would have furthered the Carbonite's cause." She skipped to keep up to Cyril's long stride. "Does Dr Webb really need me?"

"I'm not sure. I know a man has cut his leg on a furrow blade, so I used that as a reason to interrupt. Otherwise, I'd have thought of something else."

"Are you joining the Carbonites? Mathew says you are a good man, and he's a bit wary of people so that's a real compliment."

"I said it on the spur of the moment, but the more I think about it, the more I realise it's what I want to do." He touched her arm and stopped. "I'd really like one of these pendants. Where did you get them from?"

Calista smiled at his enthusiasm. "Mathew says that Father brought them from Poland. He kept them in a lead-lined box so the electronics weren't destroyed by the electromagnetic pulse. The actual devices are tiny but he had them buried in greenstone, or pounamu as Māori call it, and made into pendants. I've no idea how many he has" She lifted hers. "They are solar charged by these fine silver filaments. See?"

Cyril lifted Mathew's pendant and studied it. "The filaments look like a decoration."

"They do, and each pendant is different. You only have to leave them in the sun occasionally to charge them."

"What range to do they have?"

"About two miles, or just over three kilometres, Mathew says."

"Very handy. I'll ask your father about getting one. I may have to earn it." He grinned and tucked the pendant back into his shirt.

"I think you already have, by saving me from the squire's attentions," Calista said as they resumed their walk.

They reached Will Jasper's office and the nearby medical hut where a group of people stood outside the closed door. "Let's go in and see if you can help. A pretty face might make the injured man a little braver. There was a bit of squealing going on earlier."

Inside the small room several men, including Dr Webb, were gathered around a man stretched back on an old couch, his leg propped on a stool. Bloodied bandages lay in a heap on a nearby table, and Dr Webb appeared to have been bathing the injury, a bowl of bloody water on the floor and a red-stained cloth in his hand.

"Can I help? I do a fine line of stitching, according to Dr Elizabeth," Calista offered, purposely sounding cheerful. The men stepped back and the injured man attempted a brave smile. Pale from loss of blood, he looked close to fainting, which might be a good thing. The sliced calf muscle hung in a strip, the bone exposed in one place. It would be painful to repair.

"Does anyone have any alcohol?" she asked. The collective group wouldn't meet her gaze, eyes and heads averted.

"I've already cleaned the wound," Dr Webb said.

"Any sort of alcohol will do. Whisky, rum, moonshine, even homemade wine?" She managed to catch the gaze of one man, who gave the slightest of nods. Of course, drinking was forbidden on the farm. She'd forgotten.

She stepped close to him. "Could you please bring it? I need him to drink it. I'd like to deaden his senses so I can stitch it up. If we don't fix it properly he'll never work again." That did the trick. In these times, if a man couldn't work he couldn't support his family. The apparent leader of the group slipped away out the door and returned minutes later, withdrawing from his jacket a dusty bottle, almost full of alcoholic beverage. One whiff confirmed its strength. She looked around for a glass and one magically appeared from someone's pocket.

"Right, Dr Webb, shall we do this?" She handed the full glass to the injured man and they waited as he drank it. She then refilled the glass. "You might like to sip some while we fix you up. Could be a bit painful" He tried to smile but it looked more like a grimace, and his eyes watered either from fear or the strong drink.

"Would you like to start?" The doctor had been very quiet. She kneeled beside him and saw him shaking slightly. Surely he'd seen this sort of thing before? No, he was suppressing laughter. "I think you'd better do the deed," he whispered. "I've had a broken night feeding Daisy. Your hands will be steadier than mine."

"What's funny?" she whispered back.

"You are. I've never seen a woman boss around a bunch of burly men before, not to mention getting them to give up their illicit supply." He handed her the fine needle and thin silk thread. "I'll hold the flesh together, you stitch."

And that's what they did, for about an hour, with Calista working in close neat stitches, gathering the torn edges together, closing the wound to prevent an infection getting in. By halfway through their patient had passed out, which made the balance of the surgery a lot easier and quicker. Their audience drifted away shortly after they began and the bottle of spirits magically disappeared with them.

Chapter 7

It was two days later that Dr Webb requested Calista's assistance again. He appeared at the door to the school room where she and Mrs Grayson were teaching the children how to write their names. The first they knew of his presence was when the room stilled, and all the children stopped talking. When she looked up from the story she had been reading to Caleb, Dr Webb's rotund figure and wide grin greeted her, his finger beckoning.

Calista stood and leaned over to whisper, "Excuse me, Mrs Grayson, Dr Webb wants me."

"You go. I'll carry on with Caleb." Wendy Grayson took the book from Calista and slipped into the chair next to Caleb. The rustling of crayons on paper began again as Calista made her way around the three small groups of children sitting on the floor. For some of the farm children, school each day had become the highlight of their lives. They needed little supervision to copy the alphabet or learn to write their names. The older children took on supervisory roles as easy as slipping into old shoes; too young to labour in the fields or the kitchens, they were expected to mind their younger siblings while their parents worked.

"Do you need me?" she asked, keeping her voice low. Perhaps another accident had occurred.

"Yes and no." A familiar turn of phrase from the good doctor. She waited for him to explain. Instead, he took her hand and led her along the path toward the big house, talking as they walked. "I'm not sure how to put it, but I would feel easier, in a professional capacity, if you would accompany me during my next visit." He released her hand and stopped. Holding her gaze, he continued: "Mr Saville has requested I examine his wife, who is still experiencing discomfort and nausea. He tells me she is reluctant to see me but I feel I should do as he asks. After all, we are here at his pleasure. We're eating his food and filling his beds, while we wait for the Carbonites to return from the mountain with the solar panels."

She nodded. "And you think Mrs Saville might refuse to see you, or worse, accuse you of incorrect behaviour when examining her?"

The doctor scuffed the ground with his foot, looked around and finally met her gaze "You are a perceptive young lady. Yes, I'm concerned if I see her alone she may find a reason to besmirch me." He rubbed the end of his nose and added: "I hope I'm totally wrong, but from the brief encounters I've had with the lady I get the impression she is a bit of a princess and is thoroughly enjoying her position of power. At present we are at her mercy, too, so I need you as support, as well as a witness."

"Two against one from a witness point of view?"

"Yes, and as I can't refuse Castor's request without offending him, I am probably going to offend his wife."

"Between a rock and a hard place, then?" She reached and patted his arm. "Don't worry, Dr Webb, we can do this. Lead on."

He didn't seem to share her amusement, but together they walked up the steps to the front door and climbed the long staircase to the upper floor. The same stairs she'd fled down almost a year ago, running from Castor's advances, saved by her father and Mathew's intrusion into the bedroom in response to her frantic calls on the pendant. She buried the memory, refusing to allow it to upset her again. *That was then, this is now,* she told herself— and she now knew so much more about life outside than she had then, fresh from the tunnels and "green as grass", as her mother would have said.

They stood together and the doctor knocked firmly on the door of the very same guest room she had been assigned on her previous visit, even if she'd ended sleeping on hay bales that night in the barn with the horses.

"Come," a voice called, stopping her recollections.

Doctor Webb opened the door, stood back to allow Calista to enter and then followed her in, accompanied by a gasp from Josephine Saville. Her riot of auburn curls were held back from her face by a lime-coloured band which highlighted her green eyes. Her complexion was pale, her lips lightly glossed and she looked quite magnificent. Calista wondered if this woman had the bad temper which famously went with being a redhead.

"I was expecting my maid." Her mouth pursed and her brow creased. "What are you two doing here?"

"Your husband is most concerned, Mrs Saville. He has asked me to attend to you and see if I can find a remedy to ease your sickness." Doctor Webb indicated Calista. "Miss Waterman has some experience with natural remedies and perhaps between the two of us we can make you feel better." His tone so polite and his smile so charming, it would be hard for anyone to take offence. Calista watched conflicting emotions race across the lady's face as she fought with the desire to be rid of both of them, but also seemed to be enjoying the attention.

"I'm fairly certain I know the reason for my discomfort, but you may examine me if you wish." She moved out of the easy chair by the window and walked to the bed. She moved with grace despite being so tall. "Would you like me to lie down?"

"If you could just sit on the side for a moment, I'd like to check your pulse and vitals."

Calista moved to the window and looked out onto the grounds, admiring again the huge oak tree out the front. Its new leaves were the brightest of greens. One of the farm hands said they'd raked up the acorns and used them for animal feed but she would hunt for a few to take home and plant in Quake City.

Behind her the murmur of voices continued.

"Calista." She turned back at the doctor's call. "Could you please help Mrs Saville undress to her underwear and cover her with a sheet? I shall wait outside until she is ready."

It only took a few minutes to lift off Josephine's dress and petticoat and hang them over the dressing chair. Once she lay demurely under the sheet Calista opened the door to the hall and beckoned the doctor back inside the room. "Stay near," he murmured as he passed her in the doorway.

And so she stood at his side and observed as he gently pressed Josephine's stomach, asking if any areas were tender. Next, with the lady's permission, he examined her breasts, sat her up, and listened to her lungs and heart. Finally, he nodded and left the room while Calista helped her redress.

On his return, Josephine seated herself once more by the window.

"And what's your verdict, Dr Webb?" Her manner was a little dismissive. "Do you know why I am having trouble keeping food down and why I'm feeling exhausted?"

After a small silence the doctor said, "Yes, I do—and I'm sure you do as well, Mrs Saville."

"Please call me *Josephine*. All this 'Mrs Saville' is so formal." She blessed them both with a smile. "And what is your conclusion?"

"You are pregnant, Josephine. Possibly eight weeks, and you are suffering from morning sickness with its related periods of sleepiness and nausea—and I note your breasts have already begun to change in appearance."

A small smile lifted one corner of her mouth. "My husband will be delighted, of course, but"—she paused for a moment, and seemed to resolve something in her own mind before her face hardened a little and she continued— "I would appreciate your confidence for some time. Perhaps not *eight* weeks. I wish Castor to believe this child to be his—but..." She didn't need to add anything more for Calista to realise that the child Josephine was carrying might not be Castor Seville's.

The woman's gaze roamed from the doctor to Calista and back. Each nodded their agreement.

"The next child certainly will be his, but we have not known each other long enough, in a carnal sense, for me to announce my joyful news. I insist you tell my husband I have a mild stomach upset and I will gratefully accept any infusion Ms Waterman prepares. It might help."

"And when the child arrives early?"

"It will be 'premature' and I may also need your confirmation of that if you are attending the birth. However, I'm not sure whether I shall need you, or if you would get here in time, considering the distance you will have to travel."

Calista could not hold her tongue at the woman's suggestion of conspiracy. "It's none of my business, Josephine, but as a mother I know it's very comforting to have Doctor Webb near. He delivered both my children."

"Two children—already? You don't look old enough to have one, let alone two." She tilted her head. "You must be the lass that my husband suggested he take as his second wife. Of course, I would be his only legal wife and in charge of the house."

"I declined his offer," Calista said, adding a smile to her statement as it sounded abrupt and rude, especially as Josephine had obviously considered the proposal.

The woman shrugged. "It doesn't matter one way or the other. No doubt he will continue to search for another fertile woman. He wants lots of children and I don't intend to spend my entire time being a broodmare." She looked from one to the other. "Do we have an agreement?"

"We do," said Dr Webb. "I shall report to Castor, and Calista will make you a beverage from natural herbs to ease your nausea."

"Excellent. You may now leave," she said, and rose from her chair. They were dismissed.

Josephine seemed to glide toward the door, her dress slithering along the polished wood floor, her feet hidden beneath the hem, silent in soft wool slippers. Calista pulled her gaze from the beautiful emerald silk gown. Clothing like that could tempt most women into a marriage contract—but not her. She would admire from afar and make do with hand-woven woollen cloth. As if it could read her thoughts, her cloak whispered around her neck, the collar shifted, its touch like the stroke of a fingertip, reminding her of its strength and magic.

Wallace Howe's emotions oscillated. One moment a sense of privilege swept through him when considering his luck at being in Queenstown when the quake struck. The next moment dread filled him. What would he do now? His position of power within the Erewhon Community had been wiped out, along with the corridors and ceilings of his home. From radio reports Erewhon had been badly damaged. Most of the survivors straggling out of Wanaka exit were from Tekapo and Haast Pass, closer to Wanaka station than Erewhon.

Following a meeting of the Post Nuclear Dawn Council that morning, he walked toward the emergency field hospital in Wanaka, to meet survivors of Erewhon and the other two communities down the line. He dreaded to hear their news, knowing his worst fears could be confirmed. His two fellow community leaders probably hadn't survived. If they had, they would have managed to contact the PND Council by radio from the mountain top above Erewhon.

Worst still, his two children and his prize breeder were among the missing, presumed dead. What did he have to live for? No descendants, no power and little in the way of useful skills. There were already too many men jockeying for too few positions in the administration.

The sun shone and warmed his back. The breeze seemed stronger today. The quake had cracked the Dome beyond repair and the wild, cold weather was leaking in, along with more radiation. The Council had voted yesterday to keep the damage a secret. A mob of terrified people was beyond the best management skills of their public relations personnel. The aftershocks were causing fear enough. The lie must be maintained. The Dome protected them, kept out the radiation and regulated the weather. The truth would leak out soon enough.

The single storey building, its plaster sides cracked and dirt-riddled, didn't inspire a feeling of health and wellbeing. The old maternity annexe had been quickly spruced inside to house survivors. He climbed the three concrete steps and pressed the bell beside the open wooden door. A loud buzz echoed from down the hallway and a moment later the matron bustled up to greet him. His swing tag displayed his authority; she noticed it with a glance and her body language changed from officious to welcoming. She smiled and extended her hand.

"Mr Howe, good to meet you." Her firm grasp wrapped his hand. "What a nice surprise. How can I help you?"

"I'm here to see the survivors of the communities from within the tunnels. I've heard there are quite a few?"

"Of course, please come this way," and she indicated he walk beside her down the corridor. A glance to the side at each doorway showed people in beds with limbs suspended and heads bandaged. Noticing his glances, Matron said, "These patients are not able to talk at present. Many are badly injured and suffering from blood loss. It has taken some of them three days to reach the main exit, stumbling along twisted tracks and over rockfalls. Luckily, streams were running through the ruins here and there, so they were able to drink. However, most of them are in a bad way and fortunate to still be alive."

They turned a corner and walked along another hallway. "I'm

taking you to those who can talk. Some are almost incoherent from what they've experienced—and what they saw befall their fellow residents. We are still piecing their stories together, but it must have been horrific." Matron took a deep breath. "Please try and show no surprise at their injuries. It doesn't help recovery to know you are disfigured. There are no mirrors in here. Many have burns that are now infected. We may still lose them." She pushed the doors open and led him into the community lounge.

Around the walls and grouped around small tables, the survivors sat on a variety of chairs. Some even seemed to be sleeping, their heads slumped to the side or resting on the furniture. Wallace swallowed and noted again how lucky he was not to have been home when the quake struck. His gaze roamed the room, looking for a familiar face. To his left were a husband and wife he knew and he approached, forcing a smile, hoping he looked pleased to see them. *If only he could remember their names.*

"So glad to see you. Thank God you survived. How are you?" Obviously, they were in a bad way. Their limbs were wrapped in bandages. The smell of burned hair tickled his nose when he moved closer and his heart twisted with sympathy. Through scorched lips they mumbled their greetings, but they were not interested in talking to him. He began to walk around the room, pausing at each person to say a few words, whether he knew them or not. He listened to their stories of survival, marvelling at the strength of the human spirit to survive against all odds. He gathered from their tales that the train system through the mountain range would never be repaired. The dead would stay where they were and he hoped some of the tunnels' residents had known how to find the exits in the mountainside. The fact that the community committees had restricted the knowledge of these exits to a select few now seemed a dreadful mistake.

He ended up repeating the same words, over and over. "So glad you survived. Can I do anything for you? Do you know of any other survivors? Have you told Matron your names?" There were nods and often silence to his queries. Their gaze would meet his and slip away to look at some distant spot over his shoulder. Matron's comments rang true: many had no wish to speak of the tragedy they'd survived.

And then, after almost circling the room, in the last group he recognised Eleanor Waterman; the grandmother of his two children. His heart leapt, almost climbing into his throat. Hope filled him: perhaps they'd survived. Then she met his gaze and recognition flickered before she looked away, her head turning as if to avoid seeing him again.

"Eleanor. Mrs Waterman. Do you remember me? I'm Wallace Howe, I'm the father of your grandchildren. Do you know where they are? Are they safe? Is your daughter safe?"

She shook her head from side to side, not stopping, and his stomach roiled. Surely not? They couldn't be dead. "Will you talk to me?" He grasped her hands, wanting to hold her head still so she had to look at him, but he could see her state of mind was fragile. He knelt in front of her and waited. He had all the time in the world and he had to know whether her answer would destroy his future or not.

Minutes later she gave up avoiding his presence and began to talk.

"I didn't go. I couldn't go outside." Her voice wavered and a tremble shook her body.

"But you *are* outside. You're here and you're safe." This didn't seem to ease her tension "Where are your grandchildren?"

"They're gone. I didn't go. I'm frightened of the outside." Tears trickled down her cheeks and he wanted to brush them away, but she took a grey piece of cloth from a pocket and wiped at them, spreading the soot across her face. "They're gone. I've lost them."

Feeling confused and desperate for clarity, he risked upsetting her. "Are they dead? Did they get killed in the quake?" She shook her head and a thread of relief eased the pain in his heart.

"They went the night before. Calista, Caleb and Vanily. Gone through the exit."

"On their own?" He couldn't believe his breeder would chance that alone with the children.

"The doctor went too—and lots of others. I should have gone. I tried, but I couldn't."

Finally, he understood. He remembered that she'd been born and bred in the tunnels and, like many others, she had an inbred fear of the outside—no thanks to the policies of the PND Council.

"So Calista and my children weren't in the tunnels when the quake struck?" She nodded "Do you know where they might be now?"

It took a few moments as she appeared to be gathering her thoughts. "She's with Mathew. She will be with the Carbonites, wherever they are."

His spirits lifted. Now he had a purpose in life: to find his children and his breeder. This Mathew fellow might be a Carbonite too. They were a funny lot and he wasn't going to have his children reared by them. Somehow he'd have to get transport north.

"Would you like to join them, Eleanor? Would you like to be with your family again?"

She pursed her lips and thought for a while. "Hmm, I would, but I don't like being outside. How can I get to them? The tunnels are broken."

A nebulous plan formed in his mind. Her confusion could work to his advantage. "If I can get a covered wagon, do you think you could manage the journey?"

She gazed down at her bandaged legs and feet. "I can't walk far, my feet are broken."

He needed her with him to get access to the Carbonites. Surely she had sway with her renegade husband? Saving Aaron Waterman's wife would almost certainly give him access to his children. "It might take me a while, but if you stay here and get better I will find a way for both of us to go north. Agreed?"

She looked at him and her gaze skittered away again. He wondered if she really understood what he wanted to do. Never mind, he had money. All he needed was time to find a horse and a covered wagon, get supplies, and then he'd simply walk her out of here whether she liked it or not.

Chapter 8

Mathew shaded his eyes against the glare of the midday sun. From where he stood, the sea to the east glistened like a silver ribbon. He imagined he could see the farm where he'd left Calista, the main house a white dot in the distance, but he knew it was his imagination.

After a day to get there, one more to cut a path up the mountainside and two days to shift four solar panels down to the bottom, Mathew hoped this would be the last time he had to balance on this ledge.

"Hey, Mathew, stop dreaming. There's work to do," one of the solar engineers called to him. "The ropes are attached. We just have to lower this one and we've finished." They'd left the largest one until last.

"Thank heavens for that," Mathew muttered and reached to grab one of the ropes tied on his side of the panel. His shoulders and arms ached from days of taking the weight as they slid each one carefully downward. The rest of the rope lay curled at his feet like a mile-long snake and he stepped clear. To get tangled in that would be fatal. The first panel had squashed a path through the sparse growth which the others followed, but the previous four panels had removed the topsoil and now this one would be sliding on shale. They couldn't afford to let it go, even for a moment. It was like lowering gold-plated treasures down the mountainside, and the exercise had taken its toll on each of the five of them balanced on this ledge. Two men stood on each side and one in the middle, each with a rope to slowly feed and guide the panel to the bottom.

"Ready to release?" The call echoed against the bare rock behind them. He nodded, bracing his legs, preparing to take the weight. In the middle, a workmate levered the bottom of the panel outward, inching it closer to the precipice. It shifted, like a boulder about to roll. Everyone knew their job. Each long rope had been tied at intervals to pinions hammered into the rock wall. This would prevent the panel from taking off and sliding the whole way down and smashing at the bottom. They all hoped the pinions would hold on to this, the last and largest of the panels.

"Let her go," came the call from the far end, and the panel began to slip. Mathew turned to check his workmate beside him was standing braced and ready. At that moment a gust of wind whipped along the mountainside. It lifted the panel at the far side, tipping it up and sliding it along. The edge caught Mathew's hip and pushed him sideways. His feet slipped from under him. He flailed, the rope slipping from his grasp as he grabbed for the edge of the panel, desperate for something to stop his fall. The panel swung back at that moment as the wind died. His fingertips brushed the edge as he slid, plunging over the edge into nothingness. He spread his arms searching for handholds, his heart pounding in his ears, fear rising in his throat. Was this how his life would end? What a waste! Regret swamped him as his slide quickened, his heels digging in but unable to halt his ride to oblivion.

Then, like being slammed in the gut, he was stopped by the safety rope attached to his waist. He'd forgotten about it—and to think, he'd nearly refused to wear it! His fellow workers had shamed him into agreeing, vowing they wouldn't work with him unless he put it on. The rope circle slithered from his waist to his chest and he wondered if he'd die from whiplash or being unable to breathe. Shouts interrupted these thoughts and he looked up. Above him hung the panel, suspended with flimsy hemp ropes. They looked too thin to hold it. Its bottom edge seemed frighteningly close. If it fell it would crush him.

He looked up but the blue sky of the morning was now sliced with grey clouds. To the north the storm front covered the horizon, marching ponderously closer, its dark curves swollen with rain.

"We're going to lower you down once we've secured the panel," came the call. "Can't bring you back up. Can you hear me?"

He inhaled and managed to shout "yes", and then waited, his legs dangling, his back stinging from being grazed on the shale. He hung there for what seemed a lifetime until he felt the ground sliding beneath his back. With extreme care his mates inched him down until he bounced on a gentle slope that gave him footholds. There were small trees he could grab alongside the flattened path.

"You need to move to the side, out of the way of the panel's path." The wind again swept across the face of the mountain, casting the shouts aside and making the directions hard to hear.

"Fine," he yelled and pulled himself over, scrambling into the scrubby groundcover.

"Do you want the rope back?"

"No. You keep it on for safety. Just move as far away as you can from the scree. We don't want you slipping. We have our hands full with the panel but we've tied your rope. You can't go any further."

He did as they asked, flicking his rope over the top of the spindly bushes, none big enough to divert the path of a slipping panel.

By now the group at the bottom of the hillside were all peering up at him, waving and shouting. If there were instructions, he couldn't hear the details.

He did as directed from those above They couldn't wait for the wind to drop. There was the possibility it might even build to gale force with the approaching front—and he hoped he'd moved far enough out of the way to avoid the panel if it was flung sideways by an unexpected gust. Aaron had muttered about a weather front when they'd left camp early this morning. This must be what he'd been worried about.

"Here it comes," came the call and he watched, heart pounding, ribs aching and feeling the sting of his grazes as blood trickled down his back. The panel inched toward him, a little to one side but still too close. When he edged further away the gravel rolled beneath his feet and he grasped onto a shrub's trunk and crouched. As if crouching would make any difference if the cursed thing took off or swung in his direction. He wanted to close his eyes until it passed by and gave in to the temptation. No one could see. With his eyes closed, he concentrated on breathing, trying to ignore the stinging pain now making itself known in his palms and elbows. He couldn't loosen his hold on the shrub, not for a moment, until his nemesis had passed him by.

The rolling scrape of ravel grew louder. He risked a peep. The panel was level with him, almost within touching distance. He checked the top of the bushes he'd crouched amongst but they were still. The wind had stopped its rush along the mountainside. Moments later the top of the panel disappeared from his sight. Once it was past him, the men above were less cautious and appeared to be lowering it faster. The noise faded and he stood on shaking legs watching it arrive at the bottom. The group gathered around, like ants around a morsel, and work began on untying the ropes and loading it onto the largest dray.

"Do you want to come back up or slide down?"

He didn't know. He just wanted to get off this damned cliff-face and never have anything to do with mountains again. "Whatever's easiest," he replied.

"Probably down. We'll feed the rope out slowly, so you can make your way down through the scrub. You might slip on the panel-slide." What an understatement that was! He nodded and then realised they couldn't see him nodding, and shouted, "Okay, down it is."

At the bottom, the level ground seemed like a miracle. His legs trembled as shock set in. He'd survived when he could have been killed.

"Are you all right, son?" Aaron put his arm around Mathew's back and he flinched. "Sorry. Your back. We'd better have a look and see if we can put something on it." With that, Aaron peeled the shirt from Mathew's back and whistled a low note. "Bit of a mess. You didn't take the easy path down."

"It wasn't intentional," Mathew pointed out. "I have some of Calista's ointment in my bag. If you smear that on it later, I'm sure it will help."

"Once we've bathed all the dirt out, we'll do that. Lucky that was the last panel."

"Even if it wasn't there is no way I'm going up that mountain again, for anyone or anything. It's too dangerous. Damn the panels. I need to put Calista, the children and our unborn child first."

"Your what?" Aaron's eyebrows shot up. "Did you say 'unborn child'?"

That was a bit of information Mathew hadn't meant to let slip. He blurted it out without thinking. "You have another grandchild on the way, Calista and mine." He smiled, relishing the fact he was alive and could imagine the delicious joy of becoming a father. "I thought Calista could tell you, but I think the fall has addled my mind. All I could think of as I fell was what a dreadful waste it would be if I didn't live to see my child."

His future father-in-law laid his hand on his shoulder. "I have to thank you for many things, son. Bringing my daughter and grandchildren out, going back into the tunnels to look for Eleanor and survivors, and now you present me with more great news. I couldn't be happier." Aaron scratched his head and added, "But I have to say that Calista is only nineteen and this will be her third child. I do hope you are not going to have a fourth anytime soon."

This from a man who had three children himself! There wasn't any answer to that, so Mathew didn't bother.

Fat drops of rain hit the solar panels on the wagons. Like frogs jumping in a pond, they plopped intermittently for a few minutes. The musty smell of rain on warm earth drifted on the breeze, and then the downpour arrived in earnest. The horses raised their heads from grazing, looked about, turned their rumps into the weather and continued to graze. Their work would begin in the morning.

While the others wrestled with the final panel and loaded it on the wagon, Mathew headed for the communal tent. The rest of the day would be devoted to everyone securing the storage batteries on the third wagon. The lithium-ion batteries, which had been retrieved first, were as precious as the panels. One without the other would be useless.

Mathew wanted nothing more than a hot drink and a lie-down. His immediate aim was to get back to the farm, collect Calista and return to the safety of Quake City. He'd had enough adventures in the last fourteen days to last him for a long, long time.

The soft padding of feet caused Cyril to stop. The footsteps behind him also ceased. Someone was creeping up on him. He wheeled, confronting his follower. There were two of them. The same scouts who'd bullied Mathew, threatening him, wanting to take a wagon. Didn't they ever learn? He heard they'd been released yesterday after days of being shackled and forced to feed pigs and milk cows. Everyone assumed they'd headed south because they hadn't appeared at the communal dinner table. But no, here they were, creeping up on him like footpads from a Victorian novel.

He stood, spine erect, taller than both of them and broader.

"What do you pair of miscreants want? Whatever it is you can surely ask me without creeping around. I thought you'd left. Did you find it a bit cold out there last night, without a bed to sleep in?"

They sneered in reply. Like comic characters they truly believed looking fierce would work. Instead of being scary, they looked pitiful. He almost felt sorry for them; almost, but not really.

"Cat got your tongue?" That should stir them to talk. "We could stand here in silence all day but I have things to do, so I'm asking you again, what do you want?"

"I want my gun." The taller one, with the cracked ribs, took a step closer, his fists rising.

"Yeah. We need it, 'cos we're going south. Besides, it's ours, not yours," the short one added.

"Guns are illegal, I believe." Cyril kept his tone amiable. "You can have a gun, but not a gun and bullets—and you had bullets as well. Very naughty." He smiled. "Sorry, but I can't give it back."

"Where is it?" the shorter fellow whined. He certainly lacked personality.

"It's in a safe place and you won't be getting it back. I suggest you wander off and harass someone else, as long as it's no one on this property." Cyril assumed there would be other people who would find these two as objectionable as he did. One beating hadn't been enough to teach them that bullying didn't pay.

"We want our property. You stole it." The bigger scout stepped into Cyril's reach and while he should have resisted the urge, the man's nose looked too tempting. There was a healthy smack as Cyril's fist and the nose connected, followed by a howl of rage. This prompted the smaller man to launch himself at the former security man, arms wheeling like a windmill, landing useless blows all over Cyril's torso. Like swatting a gnat, Cyril smacked him about the ears, knocking him to the ground at the feet of his mate, who was bent over, holding his bleeding nose.

Before either could collect their thoughts, Cyril grabbed each by the collar and frog-marched them to Will Jasper's office, where he stood at the bottom of the steps, calling for assistance.

"Can someone help me with these two?" he shouted. "They need binding up again." Several workers emerged from a nearby hut and despite a short struggle, the pair were soon bound and shut once more in the farm's lock-up.

Will Jasper came down the steps from his office, jamming his hat on his head and reaching for Cyril's hand. "Thank you, those two will never learn. I bet they tried to shake you down. What did they want?"

Cyril ignored the question and said, "They're an unfriendly pair. I thought we were shot of them. They must have lurked around overnight."

Jasper smiled. "I had all horses and wagons locked up last night. I didn't trust them to leave. Now I'm going to make absolutely sure they go south."

"You can do that?" Cyril wondered. "How?"

They walked together toward the mill. "I'm sending a wagon south to Timaru tomorrow. I'll put them on it. Once there they can head inland to Twizel and down to the Dome, or go along the coast through the Caitlins and on to the bottom of the South Island. Good riddance to both of them."

'Sounds like a good plan." Cyril said.

"Would you be interested in going along? It would mean a lot to know my driver will be safe, not to mention the goods and the horse and cart." While Cyril considered the offer the foreman added, "I'll pay you well. I could do with a man like you to give me a hand. Sometimes I need some backup and I'm told you were a guard in the tunnels."

"With my height, working in the tunnels was almost impossible. I had no choice but to be an entrance guard. It wasn't my chosen career path, but then who gets the chance to pick what they want to do?"

Jasper stopped, held Cyril's gaze and said, "Perhaps I can help. What do you want to do with your life?"

Cyril shrugged. "I've no idea at present, except I rather fancy joining the Carbonites. They are a good bunch of people, genuinely trying to help others. I could do that."

"If you do this for me first, a 'thank you' for board and lodgings, then you could head to Quake City when you return. Not that I don't appreciate the work you've been doing around the place. Men with your height and strength are hard to come by."

They walked on while Cyril considered the offer. "What are we transporting?"

"End of season pumpkin and kumara; bags of unmilled grain to the flour mill there—and, of course, the two misfits, you can release them once you begin the journey back. Then I'll know my staff and goods aren't going to be hijacked by them."

"Are we coming back empty?"

"The wagons never return empty. There will be milled flour, always precious. Plus there's bound to be passengers, people wanting to travel north. The trading wagons are the most sought after means of transport. No trains, here on the outside."

Cyril stopped, a decision reached. "I'll do it," he said, "but answer me one thing first. What's the structure we're building? The framing is huge, using the biggest logs I've ever seen. We are working from an unnamed design plan. No one seems to know what it's for"

Jasper laughed. "It's facing north to get every smidgen of sun. It's to hold a solar panel we hope the Carbonites are bringing back. Whatever they salvage, we get the biggest and best. That's the deal Master Aaron did with Squire. They needed extra workmen and wagons, and we need more power than we produce with our small panels and the waterwheel."

"So if they get only two panels, you get one?"

Jasper nodded. "Seems harsh, but that's the way of the world."

"I can't go until the Carbonites return," Cyril said. "I promised Mathew I'd look after Calista while he is away."

"The precious Ms Waterman? The 'Squire's Desire' I call her." There was a sarcastic edge to his comment, but Cyril chose to ignore it.

"I'm a man of my world, Jasper. I won't leave until they return." Mentioning the squire's recent coercion efforts in the kitchen, it didn't seem wise.

"And so am I. As soon as they arrive I'll arrange for the wagon to be loaded to go south the next day. You might even change your mind on your return and decide to stay here. I can promise you a good life."

But Cyril was already wondering what he could barter for using his strength while in Timaru. The idea of trading rather appealed. He'd ask Mathew what would be useful in the city. He needed to see more of the world than the confines of this farm, which in many ways hinted at indentured labour.

The wagon train was spotted from the first-floor balcony. Pelly and Daphne raced down the stairs to the outside, calling out their news, ignoring Josephine's summons. By the time the horses turned into the main gate, picking up their pace as they neared home, a welcome crowd had gathered.

Calista scanned the travellers, her gaze flitting back and forth until she found Mathew. Her heart leapt and she ran to him as he stepped down onto the driveway.

"You're back, you're back." She threw herself into his arms and hugged him. He yelped and stiffened. She stepped back. "You're hurt?"

He nodded, his eyes moist and threatening to overflow.

"Where?" she demanded and took a step back. She scanned him but he wore a long-sleeved shirt and trousers. His face was unmarked.

"Badly grazed; my back, arms, elbows, hands, even my legs. I'm smothered in your ointment. They're clean. We got out all the dirt, but I'm very sore."

"Oh Mathew," she murmured and stepped into his arms, her touch soft against his cheek.

He grasped her hand and bent to kiss her hair. "I'm fine, truly. Just bruised and scraped. I fell down the mountainside while we were retrieving the last big panel. The wind caught it and pushed me over the edge." She shuddered and he tightened his arms around her. "It's all right. The others saved me. I had a safety rope on."

"But you could have died," she keened. She took a deep breath and held his gaze. "Take me home, please, Mathew. I want to go home to Quake City, to the stockade. I want to be safe and I want to see Mary again."

His finger traced the tear that tracked down her cheek, wiping it away. Their lips met and when they finally broke for a breath he whispered, "Just as soon as we have unloaded the large panel, then we can head home."

"Tomorrow?"

"I'll ask Aaron if we can go ahead with some of the panels. The solar engineers need to install one for Castor, and then they'll come to the stockade and get ours set up."

"Was it worth it?"

"Yes," he said, "we'll have plenty of power for the Doctor's clinic with heaps left over, providing the sun shines," He kissed the tip of her nose. "And I'm never going back to the mountains again—ever!"

"Neither am I," she agreed.

The crowd had dispersed from around them and the wagons had rolled on, the horses eager to feed and rest, though the animals' scent lingered. She breathed it in and enjoyed the memories it triggered, before taking Mathew's hand and leading him to stand under the oak tree in front of the main house. They stood holding hands, enjoying the solitude.

"Your father knows about the baby. I let it slip while I was distressed. He says he's pleased but he's already lecturing me about not having any more children." Mathew sounded apologetic and she squeezed his hand.

"He has three already, that we know of. That's the pot calling the kettle black."

Master Aaron was her father and she loved him like she had loved her mother. But not like she loved Mathew. Her father's tardiness in revealing his second family still rankled. He could lecture all he liked. It didn't mean she'd take any notice.

Chapter 9

Calista stood in Josephine's sitting room on the first floor of the mansion. Once a bedroom, it now hosted several armchairs, a cabinet, a large mirror and a floral arrangement on a small table by the window. Had she been too hasty in coming to Josephine with her request? It seemed a logical answer to her father's problem. Now she doubted her decision.

"Are you blackmailing me? Because that's what it sounds like." Josephine's voice had a sharp clip. She waved Calista before her onto the veranda that wrapped around two sides of the mansion. When Josephine stopped, just before the French doors, Calista turned to reply

"No, I don't think of my request as blackmail," although in a way it was. Calista looked around, making sure neither Pelly nor Daphne was near. "I'm trying to solve a problem that's causing concern to my father and the Carbonites, by using knowledge that I have, without involving anyone else."

'Let's sit here." Josephine lowered herself into one of three cane chairs grouped around a small table. Calista did as instructed. The warm morning sun hinted at summer to come and the glistening ribbon of snow that was the Southern Alps marked the line between land and sky.

"Let me recap your proposition, and tell me if I'm wrong," Josephine said, holding up her hand and ticking off points on her fingertips as she continued. "Firstly, you want me to intercede with my husband to give the Carbonites flour."

"Yes," Calista said. "We know he has plenty because there are bags stored here and he's sending more grain to Timaru to be milled. I know this because Cyril Fogarty is going as a bodyguard."

"And my husband is refusing you because he feels the one large solar panel is barely sufficient payment for the men and horses he loaned your father to retrieve all the panels from the mountain. In other words, he thinks he's supported the Carbonites enough."

Calista nodded. "He does. But Mathew could have been killed getting that last big panel. The squire has even suggested he should be given another panel, but we need the remaining four."

"And your idea is that I tell my husband I'm pregnant and will need Dr Webb for my confinement. By giving the Carbonites flour and spare produce, this will ensure the doctor will be prepared to travel here for my confinement." She paused and added, "Am I correct?"

"Yes." Calista looked away for a moment, gathering her thoughts. "I think your husband will be so thrilled that he's going to be a father he will be happy to part with the flour." She took a breath. "Plus, you must be about eight weeks by now, and will need to tell him soon, otherwise the baby's 'premature' arrival will not be believable." She held Josephine's gaze. "Surely you wish to have a doctor in attendance at your confinement? I can recommend him. He's a kindly man and a very good doctor.

Josephine pursed her lips and looked into the distance. She rested her hands in her lap. She was a picture of authority, very much the mistress of the house. Calista waited, her heart skipping. They needed the flour and produce and approaching Josephine for help had not been easy. She was using private knowledge learned as the doctor's assistant to further the cause of the Carbonites. It wasn't nice thing to do and it was a form of blackmail. Would Josephine help them?

"My husband is quite smitten with you and I appreciate your refusal to be his second wife." She pointed at Calista's stomach, "excluding your present condition which he is unaware of." She smiled. "Also, your herbal tea has worked well and I feel much better, but seeing as I am supposed to be newly pregnant I will continue to drink it for a while yet, even when the morning sickness passes."

"I'm pleased it helps."

"Mmm… As to your suggestion, I'll do my best. Yes, it's time I told him and I would like to ensure Dr Webb comes to the birth. I can't guarantee my request to Castor will work, but I'll try."

Calista smiled, relief coursing through her, "Thank you so much, Josephine. I appreciate it. I'm sure it will work." She wanted to hug this woman, who wasn't nearly as nasty or cold as she had been previously.

"This is not a thing done lightly, Calista. This is me helping you—and I want you to know that you will owe me a large favour if it works. Being Castor's wife is not going to be easy. Making him think this child is his is vitally important to my wellbeing and the child's. There could be times in the future when I will need a friend, and I'm hoping it will be you. Perhaps you will come with the doctor when I'm due?"

"If I can, I'll come. It'll depend on this baby," she patted her stomach, "and who might look after it while I'm away. It seems my mother was killed in the quakes. Mathew couldn't find her and up to now she's always looked after my babies." She stood and held her hand out, to seal their arrangement and to leave. "Shall we shake on it?"

Josephine waved Calista's extended hand away. "No need to be so formal. Sit down, Calista. We will have tea. I find it quite lonely already and I need some company. I'll be sad to see you all go." She rang a small bell that sat on the table and when Daphne appeared, ordered tea and cake for both of them. "Now tell me about your life. Castor tells me your father brought you out of the mountains and he thought you'd never go back. Whatever happened that made you return to the tunnels?"

At that moment a wagon loaded with bags trundled past the house and headed down the drive. Calista recognised Cyril's tall frame riding beside the driver, and tied to the side of the wagon were the two scouts. She pointed.

"Those two men made me return. They captured me when I arrived outside the stockade, having hitched a ride from Cheviot. They bundled me away in the dark and over the following days took me to Arthur's Pass. We caught the internal train to Erewhon Station, where they released me on the platform." She shuddered at the memory. "They never hurt me, but they were nasty and spiteful, making it quite clear they were being paid to return me to the tunnels. Wallace Howe paid them well." She watched the wagon pass through the gates and disappear, heading south. "I'm glad

Will Jasper is sending them away. I hope I never see them again."

"Why were you on your own? It's dangerous to travel alone. Where was your partner?"

"Those men"—she pointed in the direction the wagon had disappeared—"followed us to Cheviot. I'd gone inland with Dr Elizabeth to pick native tree leaves for remedies and they beat Mathew unconscious, wanting to know where I was." Guilt still nagged at her for causing him the injuries. "We were staying with Betty, and she found him. When I returned she'd already sent him back to the stockade to recover. Then she had to bribe a man to take me to Quake City. He didn't want to, and he dropped me off at the end of the street from the stockade. I had to walk the last hundred yards." She fingered her pendant. "The Carbonites weren't expecting me and everyone was away. Poor Mathew was still bedridden, recovering from broken ribs and bruised bones." The back of her eyes prickled and she rubbed her face.

Josephine reached and clasped her hand. "You poor thing, did you know you were pregnant?"

Calista shook her head. "Not then, but once I was back in the tunnels I knew. When the MICs said I had to have another baby, I said nothing. I knew they couldn't inseminate me. Dr Webb was great. He had plans of the exits and was prepared to help me escape. Then Mathew came, looking for me." She smiled at the memory. "He and Winston travelled together. Winston waited below while Mathew crawled through the service outlets and found me. It sounds boring when I tell it. You probably don't want to know."

"But I do," said Josephine. "It makes my life seem very dull, and I'm interested in what other people have to do to survive. Please, tell me the rest."

Calista paused before continuing. "Just before Mathew came we had a community meeting and there was a power cut during it. In the dark, I saw many people had 'Angel's Kiss'. I knew about it because Dr Elizabeth had shown me a patient suffering with it when we stayed with a family on our way to harvesting the herbal plants."

"I've heard of it but never seen it. Is it hard to diagnose?"

"No, but you need pitch darkness to see the glow. It's beautiful, but scary too, like a luminous halo. Their hair glows, and in severe cases even their fingernails glow in the dark." She remembered the young girl she'd seen with Elizabeth. "Dr Webb backed me up at the meeting and agreed this proved there was as much radiation in the tunnels as there is outside. Many didn't believe us. But a small group of people decided to escape with Mathew and me. We were only just down off the mountain when we were thrown to the ground. The quakes rolled on for ages and the mountain groaned and buckled. It was awesome to watch but horrifying as well."

Their conversation faltered as Daphne returned with the tea.

When she left, Josephine said, "We felt the quakes in the city, mostly tremors and rumbling and we heard the next day that one of the hydro dams had cracked. The lake level has dropped and there's a possibility of it breaking apart. Now there's less power in the remains of the national grid."

"This is why the solar panels are so important," Calista said. "We're going to build the doctor a clinic and we'll need all the solar energy we can get. I want to set up a warm house of some sort and use hydroponics to grow vegetables and herbs. The pumps are only small but they do need the power to run them. At the moment, most of our food is grown in the city centre in Hagley Park. It's a long way to travel back and forth to work for our share of the produce. Where we live, most of the ground has been wrecked by liquefaction."

"Why do you have to grow so much food?"

"We try to feed as many people as need a meal. There's a lot of poverty. Mary bakes bread nearly every day and the Carbonites deliver bread and produce to the many care homes in the area. It's just what they do. That, and fix things for people. There are a couple of solar engineers among the second party and they're coming to Quake City to live. They'll install our panels, but they're going to get your panel up and running before they come to the stockade."

"That will make Castor very happy. With the extra refugees arriving to build up our workforce, the farm should be able to produce even more grain and food. I'm still learning about the farm. My husband wants me to concentrate on the household, but honestly, I'll go mad with boredom unless I can find something to occupy my mind."

"Why not help with the administration? Are you any good with money and keeping track of things? Perhaps you could negotiate with suppliers—that sort of thing."

Josephine straightened her spine and sat taller. "I am indeed.

Behind this pretty face is a keen, calculating brain." She smiled to show she was being funny, but Calista didn't doubt for one moment that there was a lot of truth in her comment.

"Then you will be of great value to your husband."

"I intend to be more than just a broodmare," Josephine said, and for an instant, Calista saw a glint of steel in her expression. "I shall count you as my ally, Calista, and I'll speak to Castor immediately." She stood and Calista realised their meeting was at an end. As she went to walk away, Josephine touched her hand and said, "Remember, if you get your flour, then you owe me a favour."

"I won't forget, I promise." A thread of concern twisted her insides. She hoped when the time came the favour would not be too big to grant.

In the afternoon the men gathered outside the living quarters, securing the panels and shifting the batteries, around to make room for the travellers returning with them, ready for an early departure in the morning. Calista could hear their good-natured banter from where she sat in the workers' accommodation, mending a tear in Caleb's trousers. She ran through her mind who would be joining them on the trip to Quake City.

Mrs Grayson would be coming, much to the dismay of the farm children, but she wanted April to grow up in a larger community and she intended to set up another school near the stockade or teach in an existing one. Peter Tonkin was joining them. Presumed to be orphaned by the quake, he said he wanted to stay near Cyril and the Carbonites. He and Mathew had become great friends.

Pelly had always been coming with Calista and the children, despite two marriage proposals already from farmworkers. The Fletcher family was coming, but the Hagers had decided to stay on the farm, along with the other teenage boys. Cyril would come later, once he'd returned from his errand to Timaru. As far as Calista was concerned, taking those two scouts as far away as possible was the best thing Cyril could do for her.

The party would leave at first light. It would take the whole day to reach the city and home but she couldn't wait. If only they could leave this afternoon, but that would mean staying somewhere overnight and her father had dashed that notion, citing the safety of the panels and the need to have men on guard all through the night to prevent them being stolen.

Really? Were there such desperate individuals out there, or was it just her father's way of keeping control of the project? She suspected the latter, because not everyone would know how to use the panels. Plus, they were extremely heavy. Not the sort of thing you could pick up and run with.

She swallowed her desire to be gone from this place. She wanted to rush out, jump on a horse and ride away, which was stupid as she was the mother of two small children, pregnant, and didn't even know how to ride a horse. If she had a bicycle she could ride beside the wagons all the way home. That would be fun.

Her daydreams were broken when shouts rang out and she hurried outside to see what was causing such good cheer—to see Castor Seville standing beside a wagon full of bags, beaming widely, his face flushed as if he'd been drinking, which he may have been.

"Here you are, Aaron, I've changed my mind. To celebrate becoming a father I'm donating the Carbonites a wagonload of flour and produce. My darling wife has just told me we are to become parents. Isn't that amazing?" He walked to Dr Webb and grasped his shoulder. "I expect you to be at the birth, Dr Webb. My wife has requested it. I presume you will oblige? Can I book you in?"

The doctor smiled and nodded, "Just get the news to me when her labour begins and I'll ride down—as long as I'm alive and well."

"Then take good care of yourself, for everyone's sake," Castor added with a smile, but there wasn't any warmth in his eyes.

The next morning saw the Carbonites up early and on the road. A shallow fog hugged the ground and swirled around their ankles, and the dawn chorus joined the sound of footsteps as the birds began their day. The rising sun peeped over the edge of the sea and when an easterly breeze arrived the travellers hugged their coats across their chests and waited for the warmth of the sun. Castor Seville's farm was well behind them, disappearing below the southern horizon, and in front of them, the road stretched north to Quake city.

Already they'd crossed a braided river, vibrant with turquoise snowmelt and live with salmon. A hundred years before, an earthquake had broken up a salmon farm but the fish continued to return to spawn, their birthplace imprinted in their DNA. Calista's heart swelled with happiness. She resisted the urge to shout, and sang nursery rhymes instead with the children. Their high voices cut through the morning mist that lay in the hollows. Summer hadn't yet managed to banish the damp, but the promise of heat rose along with the sun.

Dr Webb trotted up to the side of the wagon, riding a small pony gifted to him by Castor Seville. The horse had appeared once the squire realised the doctor had no transport of his own. It was a pony, but the doctor was short, so they suited each other. It came with the comment "Now there is no excuse for you not to be at the birth of my child." The doctor was delighted to have his transport, and on his chest in a sling he carried his newly acquired daughter, Daisy. The constant rocking of the horse seemed to be keeping her content. She peeked at Calista from her secure binding and offered a tiny smile.

"I presume you had something to do with the sudden generosity of the squire?" Dr Webb's voice was barely audible as he leaned close.

Calista raised her eyebrows and tried to look innocent. "Why would you think that?"

"Because it seems too much of a coincidence; you disappear for an hour or so and later in the day a miracle happens. The Squire's blunt refusal is suddenly overturned into a shower of gifts—with a proviso, of course. I'm happy to oblige but I wonder what obligation you may have to fulfil. I doubt the lady in question does anything without payment."

"All I'm going to say is whatever I did, if indeed I did anything, I did for benefit of all of us. If it gets me into trouble in the future, so be it. I'm not admitting to doing anything at all and I would never divulge to a third party anything I heard when assisting you."

"Then whatever you did—or may not have done—I'm pleased you found a way to use your knowledge without breaking any confidences. Well done, very clever. I shall continue to trust you as my assistant." With that, he smiled broadly and trotted off to the front of the cavalcade. He, too, seemed in a hurry to reach their destination and begin his new life as a doctor in Quake City.

She watched the wagon in front where Pelly rode, chatting to the children, keeping them amused. Her gaze caught a rug being flung back from covering a bundle and then Daphne sat up, shaking her head and laughing.

"Can I come out now?" she called, and Peter Tonkin ran over

and hauled himself up the side of the wagon to sit beside her.

"I reckon we're far enough away," he said.

Calista looked at the three youngsters, their smiles, their air of happiness radiating for all to see. Josephine would not be pleased to find her maid had absconded and Daphne's mother, Mrs Rasmussen, would also feel the loss of her daughter. It looked like Peter Tonkin had a serious admirer, with Daphne willing to leave all she knew and follow him north.

Life promised to be even more interesting in the months ahead as these young ones discovered the world outside. Calista knew the feeling. It buzzed within her again this morning. Surely her troubles were now over.

Chapter 10

The last four months had been busy for Wallace Howe. Since finding out that Calista's mother, Eleanor, had survived the earthquakes in the tunnels, he'd been plotting and planning how to retrieve his children. A timid knock broke his daydream, in which he had both his children in his arms, hugging them to his chest as they giggled with delight.

"Come in," he bellowed. His lifestyle had been altered more than he liked. Little of his present existence pleased him: no obedient community jumping to his demands, no power of influence, more work, more responsibility and less pay.

His secretary bobbed her head around the door, taking a hesitant step into his office. Her timid attitude annoyed him. No matter how kind he tried to be, she acted as if he were an ogre.

"There are two men here to see you, sir." The constant "sir" grated on his nerves.

"Well, show them in. There's no need to check with me first." A thought made him pause. "Or is something wrong?"

Madeline closed the door behind her and stepped closer. "They're a bit scruffy, sir—and smelly, if you don't mind me saying so." She took a deep breath. "I know it's not polite to say so but they look like a couple of real scoundrels, which is why I thought I should check if you want to see them."

He could imagine them polluting her pristine office. "Names?"

They won't give me any. They say you will want to see them, because they have news of"— she paused—"your breeder." Madeline's eyebrows rose, her curiosity obvious. "I said you were busy but they're most insistent.".

Excitement zipped through him. He'd spent four months preparing to take leave of absence to chase Calista Waterman and retrieve his children. This could be news of their present whereabouts.

"Then I'd better see what they want. You can show them in."

She nodded and scuttled out. He cleared his desk of papers, throwing everything into drawers, and stood ready to greet the unknown, odious strangers. Better to be prepared for confrontation than to be sitting passively behind a desk, presenting a ready target for anyone with a grudge to share. He'd experienced some aggression in the past weeks. Stressed people were inclined to shout and throw their fists about, expecting him to wield power on their behalf. He refused to admit to them that his influence had faded under his new circumstances.

"No need to show us the way. We'll find him." The gruff voice had a familiar ring to it but Wallace couldn't quite place it. The door flung back, banging the wall, and standing in the doorway was the taller of the two scouts he'd hired to bring his breeder home.

"Charleston! What a surprise." Quickly following him in was the smaller, rat-like scout whose name seemed a joke of nature, "And Biggs is with you, I see. Still together, then." He beckoned them in and indicated they sit on the chairs in front of his desk. He walked back to his desk and sat, no longer afraid. These two could only want one thing—money in exchange for information. "You have news for me?"

Charleston crossed his legs and leaned back in the chair "We do indeed. Good news and valuable at that. We knew you'd want to know where your breeder is now."

"She's as lovely as ever," Biggs added, licking his lips.

A waft of sour sweat drifted toward Wallace's desk. By the look of the pair, they had been on short rations as well as a scarcity of ablutions. An air of poverty hovered about them and he could understand Madeline's reluctance to have them in her office, let alone in the building. Better to get the negotiations over with quickly and move them on.

"And my children? How were they? Did you see them?"

"Two bonny kids. The little girl is particularly pretty. Takes after you," Biggs said with a sly wink, which only served to irritate Wallace, not please him.

"Well, out with it. Tell me where they are now and anything else you know."

Charleston raised his hand and rubbed his thumb and first finger together.

"I'm well aware I need to pay you for the information. When have I ever let you down? It will depend on how old your information is and if it's worth anything, before I pay."

"It's worth plenty," Charleston said, "We've travelled miles to reach you. Lucky we all survived the quakes isn't it, Mr Howe? You, Biggs and me, we're a good team."

Wallace restrained a shudder at the thought of being part of their team but agreed on their good luck. "Yes, by pure chance I had a meeting to attend in Wanaka that morning. Very lucky indeed. My two fellow committee members are presumed dead. Did you see any sign of them during your escape?" He hoped he sounded concerned. In truth, he didn't miss Pengally's constant sniffing or Sanson's sarcasm. Their survival or demise had no bearing on his future.

Both scouts shook their heads. Wallace waited in the following silence, knowing he'd need to pay before he heard their news. He patted his pocket and checked he had some kiwi notes in his wallet. If they wanted more than he had on him, he'd need to go to the bank in Queenstown for it. He'd withdrawn funds yesterday to pay the wheelwright for upgrading the wagon he'd bought.

"Well?" He broke the silence. "How much are you charging for information these days?" Their price would show their desperation. His wasn't the most glorious of positions, but it was a job and paid well. A time-consuming position that required all his patience, but he dared not complain to the Council.

"One hundred kiwis," Charleston said.

"Seventy-five," Wallace countered.

"Eighty-five," Biggs said leaning forward, his hand outstretched. He received a scowl from Charleston.

Wallace nodded. "Better be good for eighty-five kiwis. That's a month's wages for a labourer."

"But you're not a labourer and we need the money to find accommodation and work," Charleston said.

"Not my problem. Your problem."

"We hear you're in charge of the quake survivors of the tunnel communities. We're survivors. We escaped from the tunnels that morning with about a dozen others. Helped them all escape, we did; and we've been through a lot to get here," the whine in Biggs' voice grated. "I bet you could find us work and somewhere to stay."

"I might. Depends on the quality of your news, so let's hear it or else you can leave now." Wallace stood as if to leave and suddenly the pair both began to talk at once.

He heard of their escape and the trudge to the farm that employed dozens of people. Their harsh treatment at the farm, for no good reason, they insisted—unlikely to be true, Wallace reflected, hearing of their eventual banishment to Timaru. From there they'd scrounged rides and walked inland along the old highway to Lake Tekapo, then down the middle of the island, through Twizel to here.

"Enough! That's not what I'm paying you for. I don't need the details of your travelogue; I want to know about Calista and my children."

"Just giving you some background, Mr Howe," Charleston said. "Your breeder was already at the farm when we got there, safely ensconced she was, with the two children. Seems they'd arrived a day earlier. A large party left the tunnels the night before the quake and were down the mountain when it struck. Dr Webb and others returned to Exit 5 to look for survivors. That's how we found the wagons, waiting for them at the bottom. We had to stand around until Dr Webb came back. No survivors but the guard from E5, Cyril Fogarty, came with him, along with a couple of young men. One of them, a young Carbonite, seemed very keen on Calista."

"They were pretty matey when we saw them at the farm," Biggs added, "hugging and kissing, like."

Wallace didn't care about that, as long as his children were safe. "Where are the children now? Do you know?"

"We heard they were heading for Quake City as soon as that mob of Carbonites finished cannibalising the solar panels on the mountain. Her dad's in charge. We left before they returned, but they'll all be back in Quake City by now. You can be sure of that."

"Where in Quake City? It's a sprawling community."

"At the stockade, of course. Ain't that where the Carbonites are stationed...their headquarters?" Biggs added.

"I'll need the address."

"That will cost you extra," Charleston said

Wallace shrugged. "I can ask around when I get there. It won't cost me a single kiwi to get the information." Tired of their aroma and whining, he peeled the agreed amount of notes from his wallet, handed them to Charleston, who always took the money. "Get back to me in a day or so. My secretary has forms you can fill in and I'll get you onto the survivor's list. I'll also need all the names of those who escaped with you. We need to keep track of our citizens, dead or alive."

He stood and walked to the door. "Make sure you have a shower before you even think about finding lodgings. My secretary will show you to this building's facilities," he said, and he ushered them out into the reluctant care of Madeline.

It had been money well spent. He would have paid more than they asked but had suppressed his delight in case the price went up. He now had news to pass on to Calista's mother, Eleanor. He'd spent the past months gaining her confidence, investing in her improved health and cajoling her with promises of a rosy future.

The frustration of fitting out a wagon to accommodate her fear of open spaces had nearly driven him mad, but he couldn't have both of them crazy. His desire to get his children drove him onward. A wagon large enough to have a small enclosed space built on it had been hard to find, and even harder to fit out. It had taken a large bite from his savings.

All worth it if he could bring his children back to Wanaka. Eleanor was an integral part of his plan to entice the children away from their mother. Surely they would remember their grandmother? She'd reared them both from babies while Calista worked. He'd need to hurry and begin the journey north as soon as possible, while the children's memories were fresh.

If he had to drug the damned woman to get her onto the wagon, then he would. At present, although her feet had healed, her mind remained fractured. She wavered between extreme longing to see her daughter and grandchildren and the fear of stepping outside the door of the hostel. At least she now wandered around the passages within the complex, but she preferred to do this in the dark. A strange woman indeed—but an essential ingredient to his plan; his "entry key" to the Carbonite's stronghold.

His leave of absence "for family reasons" had been arranged and within the week they'd leave. The trip could take six to eight weeks just to get to Quake City. Once he had his children, he didn't care what happened to her. Aaron Waterman could have his wife back.

Surely the man would be eternally grateful?

Everyone sat around the large square table in the middle of the stockade's kitchen, the heart of the house. They sprawled, leaned with their elbows on the table, and in Calista's case tried hard not to yawn. It was mid-afternoon and the heat of the January sun continued to scorch the plains of Canterbury, turning the concrete remains of Quake City into hot blocks. Their heat would continue to warm the air for hours to come, long after the sun went down.

The smell of cinnamon lingered in the kitchen, but only crumbs remained from the muffins Mary had baked in celebration. Each muffin had sported a slice of nectarine buried in the top and had been sprinkled with sugar and cinnamon before baking. Mouth-watering delicious and sweet, Calista wished there had been just one left over that she could sneak away for later, even if the sugar rush was making her sleepy.

She silently blessed the solar panels mounted on the roof, which allowed several old electric fans to whirl away in the corners of the kitchen. Their oscillating breeze wafted over the gathering and she shifted so that the cool air caught the back of her neck as it passed.

"Are we agreed, then?" Aaron Waterman looked around the room. "We'll officially open the doctor's clinic next week." A murmur of agreement followed. "We'll try and make it festive, with some fancy cakes." He looked to Mary Sutton and she nodded. "Perhaps some fresh fruit and drinks?" William and Benjamin grinned their agreement and raised their thumbs.

"I'll arrange the horse rides," added Simon.

"What about me?" Mathew asked.

"You can herd the children. It'll be good practice." Aaron had taken to teasing his son-in-law since the wedding in late October. "Besides, you have done more than your share with the building, and Dr Webb will probably need crowd control outside the clinic door."

"I've been doing that for weeks," muttered Winston from his corner of the table. "It's heartbreaking turning people away. The doctor can only see so many in a day in the temporary room by the stables."

"Don't worry about me," Dr Webb interjected. "It's my chosen career and I wouldn't have it any other way. Plus, without Calista" — he pointed at her sitting next to Mathew — "I wouldn't have coped as well as I did. I think she's earned the title of 'Practice Manager'." He beamed, happiness written on his round face.

He'd gained weight since they'd arrived. Calista wondered if it was solely because of the good food, or because he was too busy for exercise. She also wondered whether the extra hours he spent with Mary Sutton involved more than food. Perhaps affection made you fat? She couldn't tease him. She'd put on so much weight with this baby, she'd been waddling for the last few days, as her time drew near.

Daisy, now crawling and attempting to walk, crabbed her way around the legs and chairs until she reached her father. Dr Webb lifted her onto his knee, kissed her head, nuzzled her neck, and she giggled with delight. The beauty of this father/daughter relationship twisted Calista's heart when she thought of the years of affection she'd missed when her father had been banished from the tunnels. At times their current relationship bristled with unspoken thoughts whenever Aaron wanted her to go one way and she went the other. Despite this silent dissent, she'd made a friend of Angela, his common-law wife, and her half-siblings were now like cousins to her two children. What a complicated family she now lived in.

A moment of sadness stilled her happiness when she remembered her mother. Eleanor's death had at least simplified her father's current relationship, but as there was no proof of her death he couldn't legally marry Angela. It would be seven years before Eleanor's demise could be certified. Not that her father minded. When she'd brought it up he'd waved the discussion away, as if it were a bothersome fly. His attitude seemed to be 'if it ain't broke, don't fix it', so Angela continued to be his partner but had none of the kudos of being Master Aaron's wife.

At least she and Mathew had done the decent thing and married before this baby arrived. Her thoughts were halted by her father's question: "How's the school going, Calista?"

"Great," she answered, collecting her thoughts back to the present. "Wendy Grayson has more children than she can cope with. She wanted Pelly to help, but Pelly is now our receptionist at the clinic. She'd be wasted looking after children." That sounded wrong. "Not that teaching isn't a grand career, but Pelly has hidden talents."

"Who's helping Mrs Grayson?" Aaron frowned: one of his projects had veered off its predetermined track.

"Daphne is, along with one of the local girls, a lass who reads and writes well and is used to looking after children. She lives nearby and the school's finances can pay her, for which her family is very grateful."

"Where are Daphne and Pelly living? Can't have them vulnerable."

Calista laughed at the idea of the two girls being unprotected. Winston had been teaching them the art of Kempo. "They're in the hostel at the end of the street, along with Wendy, young April, and Peter Tonkin. The Fletcher family live downstairs, acting as houseparents with their brood and the Fletcher grandparents are on-site custodians when everyone is working. It's a good arrangement."

If her father had been around more he'd know all this, but she kept this thought to herself. As the demand for their "good works" increased, Aaron's journeys away increased, with food and fuel to source and mentors to foster.

The conversation moved on and her mind wandered to the future and her private plans. She needed to return to Cheviot and go bush, to collect more native herbs. It would have to wait until this baby was older, but the desire to retrace her journey with Dr Elizabeth kept her awake at night, as she relived those magical two weeks in her mind.

She'd found a book on native trees and Kyle has managed to trace and collect various plants for her. Her cherished kawakawa didn't grow on the windswept arid Canterbury Plains. When Kyle and Cyril travelled around the countryside foraging for machinery parts and spare timber they both looked for native trees whose leaves they could pluck for her.

In the city, the demands on River Avon had reduced it to a trickle, now more of a stream than a river. Its water kept the city's community gardens alive. For the rest of the suburbs, the braided rivers prevented a shortage as snowmelt continued to flow from the Alps. And the addition of the solar panels increased the power available to the stockade and the clinic. She sighed with contentment. Life with the Carbonites had become predictable and safe, but she had a desire to explore, like an itch she couldn't scratch. Only another trip away would satisfy her inner longing.

The meeting dissolved into a general discussion of events around the city and the demands on their time. She stifled a yawn. Mid-yawn, she stiffened and stilled.

Did she imagine it? No, the pain climbed to a crescendo. She breathed deeply, trying not to tense as she rode it through and waited for it to recede. Her labour had started. A zing of excitement warmed her. Never mind the pain ahead, she longed to see this new child, the creation of her and Mathew's love. Once comfortable again, she stood, excused herself and went looking for Caleb and Vanily's things. Their bags were packed, ready for their promised holiday with Angela. Mathew would take them. She didn't think there was any great hurry but this was her third labour and she knew each birth was different.

This time she would be surrounded with love and light-filled surroundings. Mary Sutton had promised to sit with her as her mother had before. She hadn't decided whether Mathew should be there. His parental responsibilities to Caleb and Vanily came first, as they'd discussed. He might have to wait with the men.

She leaned against the wall as pain rose within her, another small step closer to holding her precious baby. A love, stronger than what she felt with Caleb and Vanily, bound her to this child. Fear for the future and her health sometimes worried her, and then she'd think of Mathew and all her fellow Carbonites. The strength of their support and protection would chase away her imagined terrors.

Oops, another pain. They were getting closer and stronger. She returned to the kitchen door and with an effort stood tall, tried to look relaxed and beckoned Mathew. When he reached her side she pulled him into the hallway and whispered, "It's time. Tell Mary quietly, don't announce it."

His instant grin clashed with the frown that followed.

"Here are the children's bags." She pointed to where she'd dropped them. "Collect Caleb and Vanily from the crèche at the school and take them to Angela's. I'll see you when you return."

A spare room had been organised downstairs. She couldn't have climbed the stairs to their family suite at this moment, even if she'd wanted to. She longed to answer her body's demands and lie down. Even the polished wood floor at her feet looked enticing. Her legs weakened but Mathew's arms wrapped around her and held her tight.

"I love you," Mathew whispered. "Thank you for doing this for me."

She managed a small laugh as another contraction arrived. "Too late now to decide not to." She leaned against his chest and waited for it to pass, then gave him a gentle push. "Go—and come back quickly. I think this baby is in a hurry to meet us."

Chapter 11

The door of Calista's office swung open and hit the wall as Pelly rushed in. The baby stirred in her woven flax sleeping pod and Calista raised her finger to her lips. Pelly slowed and walked the last two steps to her desk.

"Sorry, forgot again about Jessica."

"It's okay, she due to be fed soon, it's just every minute of sleep she gets means a minute of peace for me. I've never had a baby so demanding." At two months old the infant had been consuming Calista's existence and as much as she loved the child, it was all becoming a bit much.

"Did you want something?" Calista said to Pelly's back as the girl leaned over the infant, whose sleeping pod rested on an examination table against the wall. "I guess you didn't race in here for the exercise."

"Oh, silly me. She's just so beautiful." Pelly turned and placed a piece of paper on the desk. "The messenger boy from the radio shed, dropped this in. He said it was very urgent, a message from the farm, from Castor Seville."

"Have you read it?"

Pelly had the grace to blush. "Yes, sorry, because it might not have been important at all…"

Calista smiled. "That's fine, Pelly. You are doing a great job as our receptionist and I know you have to weed the ailing from the needy out there." Pelly nodded and turned to go. "Just a minute, wait while I read it." She quickly scanned the words. "I need to interrupt Dr Webb and you may have to empty the waiting room because we could be away for a few days."

Pelly screwed her mouth around. "That won't be easy. Some people have been waiting since dawn to see the doctor."

"I know, but we knew we had to go to this birth. It's just come a few weeks too soon," she lied. "As soon as the doctor finished with his next patient, will you let me know and stop him from taking someone else into his office?"

Pelly nodded and left, leaving Calista to turn again to the business accounts and order forms. While little money changed hands these days, just a few kiwis here and there, money was still required to pay for medicines. She ran her eye down the requisition list she was due to send to Dunedin.

The Medical School's science department made tinctures and ointments from native remedies and was the only constant source of supply in the South Island. Auckland Medical School in the North Island did the same but the cost of transporting from there made it impossible. They were working on recreating an antibiotic once more from mould on cheese. She hoped it was successful. Oh, how she'd love to be there, experimenting and learning.

Dr Webb entered and grinned. "Pelly tells me we have an urgent message. Is it time?"

"It seems to be." Calista handed him the message to read. "Looks as if Josephine's labour has started and Castor is concerned. He thinks the baby is early and is worried about its survival. You have been summoned to leave immediately."

Dr Webb looked up from the paper. "I certainly have to, and it appears his wife has requested your attendance as well. Do we have everything ready?"

She nodded. "All sorted. I've packed something for every eventuality," she said, and pointed to the large canvas bag in the corner. "I have a small bag packed. Do you?"

He nodded. "I've arranged for the crèche to take Daisy during the day and Mary Sutton has said she will look after her at night." He pointed at Jessica. "She's coming?"

"No other option, I'm still feeding her. She's only 8 weeks old. I can't leave her here…as much as I'd like to," she added. The broken nights were beginning to wear her down.

"Then we'll leave in the hour. My pony will pull the small trap, but we can't overload her. We may have to stay somewhere overnight or arrive very late. I hope Josephine can hold on until we arrive. It's her first, and according to this message her waters have broken, so she may not yet be in labour. Fingers crossed." With that, the doctor left and Calista could hear him issuing instructions to Pelly, followed by a few shouts and groans from waiting patients. As she hurried through the reception area the doctor was giving the waiting room's occupants a lecture on how they were lucky he was here and sometimes he had to be elsewhere, plus they'd better not take it out on Pelly or he wouldn't see them when he returned.

From their upstairs family room, Calista watched the trickle of patients wander away, shoulders drooped, some limping and others standing around as if waiting for directions. People were ill and tired and although a few considered a doctor's visit as an outing, many were genuinely seeking relief. She grabbed her cloak and bag from the cupboard, plus the baby's bag, and hurried downstairs. By the time she'd left messages for Mathew with Mary and asked William to collect the children from crèche and school, Dr Webb was waiting for her with his pony and trap. She climbed aboard, placing Jessica's sleeping pod at her feet behind the trap's front panel. She'd feed her on the way.

The midday sun still had warmth in it despite it being March. The nights were cooler now and once they were on the main road south the pony trotted at a good pace, so much so that she wrapped her cloak around her to keep out the breeze. With Jessica sheltered from the draught, her cloak would protect both of them from anything the weather threw at them on their journey.

"I grabbed some sandwiches. I bet you forgot lunch," Dr Webb said.

"I did; in the excitement, food never occurred to me."

"You've been looking forward to this, haven't you?"

"I have, but I haven't been able to say so to anyone, even Mathew. Only you and I know that Josephine is now full term. I don't think Mathew will be very happy to come back and find I'm gone, but..." —she shrugged—"I don't really care."

"That's a bit harsh, Calista. He's a good man and he loves you."

"He does, I know, but sometimes I just want to run away and be me. Always there are children demanding attention. It's very wearying. I don't know how my mother coped while I worked. She never complained, and I miss her so much now that *I'm* doing all the mothering" She sighed, "And I'm only now realising just how much she did with the children. I never really appreciated her dedication."

Dr Webb patted her knee. "Don't feel guilty. Life is full of things we should have done. You can't go back and change anything. Besides, I find you indispensable at the clinic. You are a great help to me and everyone who comes."

"Thank you." Tears welled in her eyes and she wondered if perhaps she was overtired, or whether breastfeeding was taking too much of her energy.

The hours passed and the constant *trit-trot* of the pony's hooves lulled her. Then the smell of the sea lifted her spirits as the road wound around the coast and then over the braided rivers and inland again, moving ever southward to the farm.

They stopped to rest the pony and have an early evening meal. The wayside hotel would accommodate them if they wanted to stop over, but the doctor said he'd check on the pony and ask the stable hand how long he thought it would take to get to Castor Seville's farm.

Calista took the opportunity to sit in peace in a side room and feed Jessica, away from any distractions. She was such a nosey baby, much preferring to check out noises than to feed, which only meant she wanted more food more frequently. How Calista wished she could ask her mother for advice. Finally, she threw her cloak over the child's head, creating a dark space, and at last the baby fed properly. The cloak moulded around the infant with its usual rustling and Calista suspected it might have even emitted a soft hum. The cloak never ceased to amaze her. She should use it more often, but sometimes its existence slipped her mind.

With the child fed and winded she put her back into her pod and tucked the cloak over her. If they were travelling on, Jessica would need to be kept warm as night fell. She waited for the doctor to return and to hear his decision.

"All set. The groom assures me the pony is fine. It's been fed and watered well and seems sound. We'll carry on, should be there in two hours at the most. I met a fellow who will ride with us. He's on his way to Timaru and I suggested he stay at the farm the night." The doctor looked around to see if anyone was near, and leaned in, "He also said he'd make sure we were safe. Apparently, there are a few unsavoury types abroad. I slipped him a couple of kiwis. I'm sure Will Jasper will find him a bed."

She nodded with relief. Never had she thought she'd be glad to get to Castor's farm, but here she was hurrying to be with Josephine, to fulfil a debt she was happy to repay.

After they'd climbed into the trap and settled themselves, Dr Webb clicked his tongue to set the pony going and turned to her. "I saw a funny thing while I was negotiating with our fellow traveller." He indicated the large man astride a gelding, now riding alongside them. "I thought I saw Wallace Howe go past, heading north, driving a large wagon. It had a box affair on the front of it and was carrying a couple of passengers on the sides." He shook his head in wonder. "It looked so much like him I nearly called out, but it couldn't have been him. Surely he would have been killed in the earthquake along with most of the Erewhon Community."

Calista shuddered at the thought of Wallace Howe being alive. He might be the sperm donor of her two children—or so he said—but there wasn't anything at all attractive about him.

"Cold?" asked Dr Webb. 'Here, wrap this rug around you. I see you've used your cloak on Jessica."

She murmured her thanks and slipped the rug around her shoulders, hugging it across her chest. Sometime soon, when the moment was right, she needed to ask Dr Webb about how she could train to be a doctor, because being a mother wasn't her purpose in life. She knew this with deep-seated certainty. Motherhood had been thrust upon her three times. Never again, she vowed.

She needed to do something fulfilling with her life. She blamed her lack of maternal instinct on being inseminated against her will, twice. Surely that was enough to put anyone off mothering. She was very fond of her children and felt a responsibility for their well-being, but would she devote her whole life to them, as her mother had done? At this moment, definitely not. Did that make her a bad person?

The baby whimpered and the sound tugged on her heart. Yes, this little one had a greater pull on her emotions than Caleb and Vanily, but even Mathew's daughter wouldn't stop her from breaking free from the path the men in the family expected her to travel.

Kyle hurried into the kitchen and tapped Mathew's shoulder. "There's a big wagon outside the gates. The man wants to come in. Says he has someone called *Eleanor* with him. Says it's Aaron's wife."

"What?" Mathew stood so quickly his chair fell back on the floor, causing Mary to drop the bowl she was carrying.

"Please, Mathew, be careful. You shocked me. It's dangerous with hot things in my hands." She bent to pick up the pot that had luckily landed the right way up.

"Sorry, Mary," he muttered, and led Kyle out into the hallway. "Say that again."

"The man has a big wagon with a sort of shed on the front, which he says a woman called Eleanor Waterman sits inside. He said Master Aaron would be pleased to meet with him and grateful he'd brought his wife to Quake City. I don't know if he's telling the truth but he's adamant I tell someone."

"I can't believe it. Eleanor, alive? This I have to see. What does he look like, this man? Did he give a name?"

"Howe, he said, something Howe. He acts all important. The horse looks exhausted. I nearly opened the gate to let the poor horse in but thought I'd better check with you first."

Mathew patted Kyle's shoulder "You did the right thing," he said, and they walked toward the front door. By the time they reached the courtyard Matthew had decided he needed support if it was truly Eleanor. It could be a sick joke by someone who knew she'd been killed. He stopped and said "Could you go and get Winston to join us? I've only met the lady once and although I would recognise her, she might be in a fragile condition, especially if she's shut in a shed."

While Kyle hurried to the stables to get Winston, Mathew went to the double stockade gates and peered through the viewing hole. Yep, tired horse, long double-axle wagon with a peculiar shed affair at the front, wedged between the side seats; looked ridiculous. He waited until his fellow Carbonites joined him before he opened the side gate and they ducked through onto the roadway.

"My friend Kyle tells me you have a woman named Eleanor with you? Is that right?" Mathew pointed at the shed.

"Yes, it is. Eleanor Waterman," said the man. "I've brought her all the way from Wanaka. It's taken me eight weeks and a lot of money, but I'm sure Aaron will be delighted that I've saved his wife and returned her here in good shape."

"Why is she shut in a shed?" Winston said.

"If you knew the good lady, then you'd know she has a sickness. She's afraid of open spaces and the only way I could get her to travel was to build her a little room to hide in." The man by now had climbed down from the wagon and was standing in front of the three men. "If you don't believe me you can climb up and see for yourself. Just don't open the door too wide. She gets frightened. I would recommend you speak to her through the door. She'll be fine later. She's happy to wander about in the dark." The man stood, feet apart, his arms folded. "Well, go on, check. You'll find I'm correct, and I expect to be rewarded for my efforts."

Mathew's stomach clenched. What a nightmare; Calista away, Aaron with his common-law wife, and Eleanor here and totally crazy by the sound of it.

"And who are you? What's your name?" Winston stepped up, equally belligerent, seemingly unimpressed by the man's stance. "We hear a lot of stories being told outside these gates and we don't offer hospitality to just anyone."

The man stood tall, pushed his chest out and hooked his thumbs into his belt. "My name is Wallace Howe. I was a member of the Community Committee at Erewhon Station. Now I work for the Dome Committee. On the morning of the earthquakes I was in Wanaka and that's where I found Mrs Waterman days later, after she'd staggered out of the tunnel exit, along with a handful of other survivors." If he meant Winston to be impressed, he would have been disappointed. The Carbonites had poor opinions of any men in positions of power. All of them had heard Aaron's contempt of the MICs.

On hearing the man's name, Mathew knew life had just become more complicated. His throat tightened. Wallace Howe, the semen donor of Calista's two eldest children, who were now, by marriage, *his* own children. Although Howe said he'd brought Eleanor here in good faith, Mathew suspected he had an alternative motive: to see Caleb and Vanily.

He stepped back and murmured to Kyle, "Can you cycle to Aaron's and ask him to come immediately? We will need him to confirm it's Eleanor." Not that he doubted it, but this shouldn't be his problem. He remembered that Cyril was in the city and Aaron might be with him. "If he's elsewhere with Cyril, could you find him and bring him back?"

Kyle, ever willing, nodded, saying, "I know where they might be working," and he ducked back through the door in the gate to get his bicycle.

"Right, I'd better have a look then," Mathew said, and with a glance at Winston and receiving an acknowledging dip of his head, Mathew climbed up the back of the wagon, knowing Winston would keep a firm eye on Wallace Howe.

He knocked on the small door and said, "Eleanor, it's Mathew. Is that you?"

"Oh, Mathew, yes I'm here. Are we really in Quake City?" Her voice sounded frail and querulous. "Is Calista there?"

"She's away at the moment, helping with a birth, but she'll be back in a few days." His neck ached from bending down, so he kneeled and opened the door a few inches, only to meet resistance from Eleanor's foot.

"Please don't open the door, Mathew. I'm frightened."

His patience was already stretched and he snapped, "Well, you'll have to come out sometime and it might as well be now. You can't stay here on the wagon for the rest of the day."

"I can. I always do. You can't make me come out." Her voice had a whine and childish lilt to it.

"Don't you want to see the children?"

"Oh, yes. I want to see my grandchildren. It's been so long. Will they remember me?"

"I'm sure they will, but you'll need to come out and into the house, so you can greet them when they come home from school."

"They go to school?"

He noticed Kyle cycling away at speed, and relief eased his impatience. "Vanily goes to the crèche at the school and they're due home soon. Please, Eleanor, you've come this far, surely you can make the effort and get down off the wagon."

"I need something to cover me. A blanket, something to hide the sun."

Mathew wondered if he wanted to be bothered with all this. She could just stay there and he could return to the kitchen and Mary's sensible personality. His conscience pricked him, though, and he sighed.

"I'll be back in a moment." He climbed down, whispered an

aside to Winston, who remained on point duty watching Wallace Howe until he returned moments later with a large grey blanket. He climbed onto the wagon.

"Here you are," he said, handing Eleanor the blanket through the small gap in the doorway. He waited.

Minutes passed and he heard the piping voices of children. School was out and down the road raced his two children, holding hands with the Fletcher kids, giggling with joy, their feet kicking up puffs of dust as they ran home.

At the same time, Eleanor emerged, bent over through the shed door, the blanket draped over her. She looked like a slow-moving turtle, bent over and shuffling under her covering. He took her extended hand and guided her to the end of the wagon. By then the children had reached the wagon and stood staring up at the person draped in a blanket.

She paused at the tailgate, peering down at the single iron step she had to navigate to get down.

"Grandma?" Caleb's voice held amazement and wonder. "Is that you, Grandma?"

"Caleb, darling. You've grown so big." Eleanor reached her thin arm toward him and the small boy scrambled up onto the wagon and wrapped his arms around her legs, before turning to his sister and calling, "Vanily, it's Grandma. Remember?"

Vanily stared, a frown creasing her forehead, her blond curls bobbing as she shook her head.

Mathew looked from his children to Wallace's Howe's face, now lit with longing, his arms stretching toward the children. His gaze met Mathew's, his arms dropped and he turned away. His emotions had revealed his intent.

Hampered by Caleb's joy and his insistence on helping Eleanor off the wagon, it took a while to get her down and through the gate, along with all the children.

Mathew shepherded them before him and once he had them all through he turned to Winston.

"Don't let him in," Mathew said. "He wants the children."

"I'll move him on. You can lock the door. I'll wait here until Aaron arrives."

Mathew rubbed his face and ran his fingers through his hair. "What a mess."

"Looks like having too many wives is worse than no wives," Winston said with a wry smile.

"One is enough for me," Mathew said, and wished yet again that Calista hadn't hared off to birth Josephine's baby. Its early arrival was a worry, but did she really have to go?

Chapter 12

The door in the gate closed behind Mathew and the children and Winston continued to stand guard. A stalemate had been reached.

"I would suggest you move on, Mr Howe," Winston said. "There's a boarding house further on. You turn right at the end of the road, can't miss it. They have stables, too. Your horse looks worn out."

"I'm not leaving here until I've seen Aaron Waterman. That man owes me. I've spent a lot of money getting his wife here. Plus I want to see my breeder and spend some time with my children. They're my children, you know, not just hers."

Winston took a step closer, squaring his shoulders and holding Wallace Howe's gaze. "If I were you, Mr Howe," he said, his voice so soft Wallace had to lean in to hear, "I wouldn't be using the term 'my breeder' around these parts. Her husband might get very upset and take offence."

"Well, she *is* my breeder."

"Miss Calista is married to Mathew now, and if she's anybody's breeder she is his, not that I would use that term in front of either of them. They also have a new daughter."

"Perhaps the child is mine as well. I instructed the doctor to inseminate her as soon as she returned."

Winston shook his head. "I understand Miss Calista was already pregnant when your men kidnapped her from this very spot."

Wallace stood his ground, his face red with heat and rage. "I'm not leaving until I see either Aaron or his daughter."

The horse snorted and stamped its feet.

"Please take your horse to shelter, Mr Howe. It needs hay and water. We are lost without their service and thank you for bringing Mrs Waterman to Quake City. I'm sure Master Aaron will be most grateful, However, neither he nor Calista are here. I would suggest you return in the morning. By then Master Aaron will have come home and I am sure he will be very happy to meet with you."

The doorway opened and Mathew appeared, his mouth set in a thin line, the muscles along his jaw tight. He stood at Winston's side and glared at Wallace Howe.

"This man tells me you are married to my...to Calista," Howe said.

"I am, and the children consider me their father, which legally I am. I've adopted them."

"That's preposterous. They're mine. I can prove it. The records are there, at Erewhon. I have witnesses. Dr Webb can verify..."

Mathew raised his palms to shoulder height to stop Wallace's tirade. "Mr Howe, I've been in the tunnels since the earthquake, looking for survivors. I've seen the devastation. Have you?" Howe didn't reply. "If any record existed it was probably destroyed, and if not then there is no way of retrieving it. As far as the Court is concerned, Calista and I are the children's legal parents. If you want visiting rights you will have to discuss that with my wife—when she returns."

And with that, he turned on his heel and strode away down the road, past the clinic, past the boarding house where the other tunnel survivors lived and on toward the river. It seemed to Winston that Mathew was walking off his anger. The young man was slow to boil, but once angry he then had difficulty overcoming his desire to lash out.

"Truly, a wise man would leave and come back in the morning," Winston said.

Howe climbed onto the wagon seat and turned to shout. "I'll be back in the morning and every morning thereafter until I get what I want." He flapped the reins and the horse trudged on, ears flattened, head low. Winston thought the horse at least would be happy for a few days' rest. He wished he had an apple in his pocket, the animal looked like it needed a treat.

a heaved a sigh of relief. What bliss to be home. Dr Webb ...ed the pony and trap to a halt outside the clinic. They'd been travelling since just after dawn, with two brief rest stops, hoping to make it home before dark. Already the birds were twittering, settling for the night. Another half an hour and they would have been travelling in the dark. Not a good idea if you could avoid it.

The clinic's door opened and a small boy darted out, followed quickly by Pelly, who handed him something, and he raced off down the steps with a grin on his face

"What's all that about?" Calista asked as she climbed down from the trap, reaching to get Jessica in her sleeping pod. After being rocked asleep for so many hours today, the youngster would be wide awake now for hours.

"I've sent him off to get Mathew, to tell him you're back."

"But I can walk, it's only next door. It'll take me five minutes to get there,"

Pelly waved her fingers, "No, no. Mathew wants to talk to you here before you go home. There's been a lot happening in the past week while you've been away."

"Can I go into my clinic and sit down?" Dr Webb said, raising his eyebrows. "Or will my receptionist have orders for me as well?"

A blush rose up Pelly's neck. "Of course you can go in, Doctor. This is your clinic and your home, it's just that Mathew was most insistent... And look, here he comes."

Calista turned to see her husband hurrying toward them. Moments later she was enveloped in his arms.

"Oh, so glad you are home. Wonderful to see you. Has our baby been good?" He took the sleeping pod from Calista and with gentle pressure on her spine guided her up the steps and through the clinic door. She stopped in reception. "Mathew, what's all this about? I want to go home. Why are we in the clinic?"

"I'll tell you in a minute. How's Josephine? How's the baby? Is everything alright at the farm? Let's go into your office."

As they walked down the passage, she told him, "Josephine is fine. A long labour but a healthy little boy."

"Of course he'll be little, being so early."

She didn't answer that. Couldn't, really. "He has Josephine's red hair but is quite finely built."

"He'll grow," said Mathew, "Castor's a big fellow."

Again she couldn't comment.

He put the sleeping pod on the floor under a hanging mobile for Jessica to watch, and embraced Calista again. "I've got good news and bad news. What do you want to hear first?"

"Oh Mathew, don't play games." Her chest tightened. "Are the children safe?" He nodded. "Then just tell me the news however you like, and hurry, because I want to go home and lie down in our bed and enjoy being safe in the stockade. So what's all your news?"

He guided her to the old sofa she kept in her office, in case she ever had the chance to snatch forty winks, and they both sat. She took a deep breath to calm her nerves and noted that Mathew did the same.

"Well?" she said.

"Your mother is here." Calista felt her mouth fall open, but she couldn't comprehend what he was saying.

"Mother? Here? Alive?" Her heart swelled with delight. "How wonderful, I've so missed her. She will be so happy to see the children." Then, searching Mathew's face and seeing no matching delight, she asked, "Is she alright?" Her joy turned to fear.

"Yes, and no. She's very frail. Her feet are badly scarred from her trek along the train lines to get out, along with about two dozen other survivors. They emerged at the Wanaka end of the tunnel system." Mathew stroked her hand and gripped it. "She is not very stable mentally, but has perked up in the last few days being inside with Mary, helping in the kitchen and of course she's delighted to see Caleb and Vanily. Caleb is full of excitement at her arrival but it took Vanily a few days to thaw. I'm sure she'd forgotten her in the months since we left."

Then Calista thought of her father and his second wife. "Has Father told her about Angela and his other children?"

Mathew shrugged. "Who knows? No one is prepared to ask him. He comes every day to see her and stays for about an hour. When she asks for him, everyone says he's away working and is very busy. She never asks what he's doing."

Calista buried that worry deep. It wasn't her problem, it was her father's.

"So Mother is here and alive, that's great. What a journey—and she's frightened of the outside. She must have overcome her fear. How did she get here?"

"That's the bad news, I'm afraid."

Calista waited as Mathew picked up Jessica and laid her on his knee, patting her back. Jessica rewarded him with a belch. "Tell me, Mathew, please."

"Wallace Howe brought her. He was in Wanaka the day of the quake, and once Eleanor was well enough he had a small shed built on the back of a big wagon and brought her to Quake City. He expected compensation and I think Aaron has paid him some kiwis toward the cost, but he's demanding time with the children on a daily basis. He sits and talks to your mother and I've threatened him with ejection if he dares to mention to them that he is their biological father."

"Damn the man," she swore, "he's like a sore you can't heal and weeps poison into my life."

"He's waiting to see you. Flatly refuses to leave the city until he has spoken with you. Says there's unfinished business and even tried to tell me that Jessica might also be his." At this he put the baby to his shoulder and kissed her cheek. "I will ask Dr Webb if there's any way to clarify that."

Calista touched his knee. "Don't worry, Mathew. I'll put him straight. How dare he think he can interfere with my life now that I'm free of the tunnels and his damned influence."

She stood. "Come on, let's go home. I'm dying to see Mother. I hope Howe isn't there now."

"He comes in the mornings, sometimes before the children go to school."

"You carry your daughter and I'll take the bags," she said.

They were about to lock the clinic's front door now that Pelly had left, but Mary hurried up the steps, carrying Daisy. "I'm bringing her back to her father. He'll want to see her," she said as she passed them on the steps. "I'll lock up."

"Do I detect a tinge of embarrassment there?" Calista murmured to Mathew.

"I think there's a bit of a romance brewing between Mary and our good doctor." Mathew glanced behind to check the clinic was closed. "They seem to spend a lot of time together and I'm sure it's not Daisy alone that keeps drawing them together."

"Good for him. He's a lovely man," Calista said, "like you are." Mathew's grin wiped away the day's patina of weariness. He always made her happy—well, almost always.

As they walked to the high double gates, Calista told him of the huge wagonload of autumn fruit and dressed hogget that would be arriving tomorrow. Castor Seville was so thrilled with his son, and their attendance to Josephine, he was sending a wagonload of *thank yous*.

"Fabulous. The solar panels have been switched on this past week and the new cool room at the end of the stable block is working. We have enough power to keep the chillers running, which means more food in storage for times of need."

They ducked through the small door and at the entrance hall to the big house Calista dropped the bags and hurried into the kitchen, calling, "Mother, mother, I'm home." She hid her shock, maintaining her smile, as Eleanor rose from the rocking chair where she'd been reading aloud to Caleb. Wrapped in her, arms her mother seemed like a small bird with bones that could break if she hugged too hard. Tears blurred her sight as she stroked her mother's hair, now more grey than black. Eleanor's brown eyes holding Calista's gaze had lost their sparkle and darted from side to side as if fear lurked over Calista's shoulder.

"We have a new baby, Mother. Mathew will have told you. Look, here she is." She took Jessica from Mathew and held her up for inspection. Eleanor glanced at the child and looked away, and then sat down again in the rocking chair. "Would you like to hold her?" Calista moved to place Jessica in Eleanor's lap.

"No thank you, dear. I've had enough of babies," she said, and she put her hands up to stop the infant's arrival on her knee. She then picked up the book and began reading aloud again.

Calista's stomach roiled at her mother's sudden dismissal of Jessica. This woman now ignoring the baby's presence looked like her mother, spoke like her mother, but certainly wasn't the mother who'd cherished her children and almost left the tunnels with them, before she ran back down the passage the night they left. But perhaps she *was* the same person? Perhaps this version had been there all along and Calista hadn't recognised it. Her dreams of a joyful reunion lay shattered on the floor. She leaned and patted Caleb on the head, "Lovely to have Grandma back, isn't it?" He nodded, enthralled in the story Eleanor continued to read.

"Let's go, Mathew," Calista said, and they climbed the staircase to their family room. "Where is she sleeping?"

"In the spare room downstairs," Mathew said. "The problem is she wanders around the house all hours of the night, opening and shutting cupboard doors and peeping into people's rooms. Heaven knows what she's looking for. I might ask Dr Webb for a sedative to slip unto her evening drink. It's getting beyond a joke and she's only been here five days."

Just when you think life is good and the future plotted out, something else comes along and shatters your world. Tomorrow she'd have to face Wallace Howe but this time it would be on her home ground and she held all the cards, she hoped.

Chapter 13

Leaving Jessica asleep in their bedroom, Calista headed down the wide staircase and into the kitchen for breakfast, only to halt at the doorway. Her hand moved to her throat and she made an effort to lower it and take a long, calming breath. Seeing Wallace Howe sitting at the table, his hands wrapped around a mug and his gaze locked on hers was not the way she wanted to start the day. Too late to back out of the doorway now.

"Calista," Eleanor said, "come and say hello to Mr Howe. Without his help I'd never have made the journey. You have a lot to thank him for, and so do I." Her mother smiled at Howe, her grateful adoration making bile rise in Calista's throat. Even allowing for her mother's fragile mental state, she thought Eleanor was carrying gratefulness a bit far.

"Come, daughter. Don't just stand there. Come and say hello and at least thank Wallace for his trouble."

So now it was "Wallace", all friendly and sweet. Calista swallowed, breathed deeply and stepped forward, moving to the stove to get hot water for a drink. With her back to Howe and her mother, she ordered her thoughts and reminded herself this man no longer had any hold over her. She was free—married, and the mother of three children, no longer a teenager unsure of herself and what life held. Never again would she be at the beck and call of the Community Council in Erewhon.

She took a chair beside her mother, across the wide table from Howe.

"Thank you, Mr Howe, for bringing my mother safely to Quake City. Mathew and I are very grateful. I'm sure my father is, too.

Have you seen him?" She held his gaze, daring him to look away first, which he did. His gaze flitted to her mother and back to her.

"I've met with your father. He's a hard fellow to pin down, but we've had a chat. I've also met your husband briefly, and now I hope you and I can discuss my children."

Time to put that right. "The children are not yours. They are Mathew and my children, all signed and legal with the court. Mathew has told you this. You have no claim at all to Caleb and Vanily, or their future." She almost spat the words at him.

"Calista!" Her mother's tone was high and sharp. "That's not the way to speak to Mr Howe. He's been wonderful to me and is very good with the children. We all know they are his children. Apologise."

Calista had to remember she was an adult now and not subject to her mother's instructions. Rather than tell her mother to mind her own business, she spoke directly to Howe. "I had no say in whose sperm inseminated me when I was fourteen and sixteen. You claim it was yours. It may have been someone else's."

"It was mine." Howe's face reddened and a film of perspiration rose on his upper lip. "You know damn well it was. You are being obtuse by denying it."

"If there was a written record it is buried, along with many of the inhabitants of Erewhon."

"Dr Webb will confirm it," Howe growled.

"I've discussed this with Dr Webb. He didn't inseminate me, a visiting clinician did, on both occasions, because he ethically disagreed with the practice. He also confirmed that he never kept a record of any donors."

"The damned man is dodging the issue. The records will be in Queenstown or Wanaka. They'll be somewhere." Howe's voice had risen and Eleanor reached and patted his hand.

"Don't get overexcited, Wallace, it's not good for your blood pressure," she said.

Ignoring her mother, Calista continued. "I will give you an undertaking that should either Caleb or Vanily ever ask about their parentage I will tell them the truth: that you claim to be their father but I have no proof of their parentage because I was inseminated." Howe opened his mouth but she carried on quickly. "I think you should know that the court asked me, at the time of Mathew adopting them, if I'd like to register a charge against those responsible for inseminating me at fourteen. I said it was a decision made by the Community Council at Erewhon and I listed your name and those of Peter Pengally and Aric Sanson. I presume the other two are dead, but you are obviously not. You are liable for prosecution should I wish to press charges, now that we know you are alive and where you live. Think about that, Mr Howe, and consider whether you wish to continue to make my life difficult."

Eleanor gasped and shook her head, her displeasure at Calista's words written on her face. "Where did you learn to be so rude?"

"Life has taught me a few cold facts in the last year, Mother. Things you never told me, about the power of men and their hold over women and our bodies. Things I thought were normal, only to discover they were cruel and designed to breed workers to satisfy the desires of those in power."

"Utter nonsense," Eleanor muttered, tossing her knitting onto the floor. Her chair scraped as she stood and hurried out the door.

"She's not well," Wallace Howe said.

"I can see that quite clearly, but I suspect it suited you to bring her here, hoping to wheedle your way into my life once more. Be warned, Mr Howe: I will activate that charge if you don't get out of my life and those of my children. Just like I had no say in their conception, you now have no say in their development. They are mine!"

Howe appeared to accept defeat. He nodded. "You are doing a good job with them. I thank you for that. And your husband appears to be genuinely fond of them."

"He is. I'm lucky he feels that way. Not every man will take on another's offspring."

"True." Howe paused and after a short silence, which Calista refused to break, added, "I need to make my way south to Wanaka sometime soon. Can I continue to visit the children until I leave?"

His quick surrender took her by surprise and her mind whirled for an answer. Could he do any damage that he hadn't already had a chance to do? "How much longer will you be in Quake City?"

"Perhaps another week at the most. I need to find a buyer for my large cart. It was purpose-built to accommodate your mother's..."—he paused—"needs. Not everyone wants a wagon with a shed on it."

Perhaps not, but she knew of one such a person. "Very well, one more week and then you must cease visiting. I don't want them confused by your presence or sudden absence. I hope my mother hasn't been filling their heads with nonsense either."

"I have no control over your mother's thoughts. They can be quite addled at times."

"So I hear." She stood, returned her still full cup to the sink and turned to see Howe rising from his chair. "I'll show you out," she offered.

"I know the way by now." He walked toward the door, then paused. "What about my cloak? I'd like it back, seeing as you have my children. Fair exchange, I think."

His cloak? The one he gave her when Caleb was born? The cloak that rustled and clung to her?

"No, you can't have it. It's bonded to me. It won't hang around anyone else's shoulders, even Mathew has tried. It goes as stiff as a board if other people try to wear it. I don't know why, but it's definitely my cloak. You're wasting your time thinking you could wear it."

"Damn, I hadn't considered the A.I. thread would bond with you."

"A thread? An intelligence of some sort?"

"Yes, finer than a hair, a fibre instead of a computer chip, woven through the tyvek to make a 'thinking fabric'. My great-grandfather was involved in the experiment, just before the Nuclear Dawn. They made one bolt of material and he managed to get enough to make a cloak. It stayed in a box until you had Caleb. I was so thrilled to have a son..." He sniffed and rubbed his eyes. She almost felt sorry for him... Almost, but not quite. "I gave it to you thinking it would keep you safe and warm in the tunnels. I appreciated your labour."

So much so he had her inseminated again! But she was glad he'd given it to her, and now she knew why the cloak seemed alive. It was, in a way.

"Too late now, I'm sorry. It is truly bonded to me, but I thank you now for it, as it's kept me warm and dry on many occasions."

She walked him to the door in the gate, waited while he left and bolted the door behind him to prevent him from returning, then realised the door needed to be left open for the Carbonites to use so she slipped the bolt back. She would make sure she was up early for the next week or would skip breakfast and eat at the clinic. She hurried back inside to collect Jessica, her appetite deadened by her meeting with Howe. The children had gone to school already and as to what her mother was doing, she didn't care. Eleanor's complete lack of interest in Jessica hurt, like a blade in her heart, every time her mother rejected the baby.

At the end of that day, the residents of the stockade gathered in the large lounge after the evening meal. Calista noticed that Dr Webb chose to sit next to Mary, Daisy scrambling between their knees. Her father arrived just as everyone found a seat. Caleb and Vanily played a game of dice on the floor near her feet and Mathew leaned against her shoulder, weary from his day in the gardens. She smothered a yawn and hoped the meeting would be short, which it was. The only matter of importance was the constant problem of finding food, storing food and getting food to the poor. Castor's wagonload had been portioned out and what could be chilled now filled the cooler.

As the meeting broke, she sidled up to her father. "Can I have a few words, Father?"

"I'm rather busy, daughter. Does it have to be now?"

"Yes," she said. "Now is good. We're all busy." She tugged his arm and he followed her to a side room often used for storage. She could sense his reluctance but she had things to discuss. She closed the door behind them and turned.

"I had a meeting with Wallace Howe this morning."

"So I heard from Eleanor."

"From Mother?" He nodded. "Well, she wasn't any help. I said I'd tell the children of his claim to parenthood, if they ever asked, but most importantly I threatened him with court action if he ever interfered with my life again."

"Good girl. Now can I go?" He reached for the door handle.

"No." She held his jacket. "Have you told Mother about Angela? Everyone wants to know and no one else is prepared to ask you. Mother keeps asking where you are and your friends are tactful and say you're busy. It's not fair on all of us. It's lying by omission and we don't enjoy it. You surely have to tell her."

"Why?" Her father's raised eyebrows and casual shrug annoyed her.

"Because it's not fair on me, or Angela—and what about Colin and Belinda? Caleb and Vanily are missing their company."

He stiffened and his brows met. "It's nobody's business but mine. Your mother is an adult. At present her brain is like scrambled eggs and she is not interested in being a wife to me again. She doesn't even want a cuddle. I'm sure she'll eventually work out that I have another family." He grasped the door handle again. "When she does bring it up, then I'll discuss it with her. Meanwhile, everyone can continue as they have managed to do since she arrived."

Before she could think of an answer, he left. By the time she gathered her frustration and swallowed her anger and then stepped into the hall, he was gone. The need to find Cyril took over and she found him in the kitchen, raiding the larder. He'd missed dinner because he'd been delivering to the care homes in the suburbs.

"Cyril, just the man I want to see. Do you have a minute?"

"I've all the time in the word for you, my dear. What can I do for you?"

"I think I've found you a wagon. Remember you mentioned starting a carrier service between here and Timaru, hopefully taking parcels and passengers?"

"I did, and I'm still looking."

Satisfaction warmed her and she grinned. "I've found you a wagon, possibly a horse too."

"You have? You beauty," and he picked her up and swung her around, carefully placing her back on the floor. "Who, where and how much?"

She laughed. "You'll have to negotiate with him but Wallace Howe is looking to sell his wagon. It has that shed affair on the front that Mother hid in on the trip up. I thought that would be great to lock parcels in, and there is a bench seat down each side. He brought some people with him as paying passengers." Cyril nodded. "And you could arrange overnight accommodation on the way, and charge more perhaps, taking your time on the journey. What do you think?"

"Sounds ideal. I know where he's staying, I'll see him tomorrow, but buying the horse is doubtful. Winston mentioned it was lean and poorly."

"I don't think Howe knows a thing about stock, so you might be able to get the horse thrown in, and then build up its health and use it as a spare. Mathew might know where there is a strong horse for sale."

"I'll follow it up. Thank you, Calista. When is Howe looking to leave?"

"Not for another week, but if you offer to take him back as far as Timaru he might leave earlier."

"Sounds like you're in a hurry to get rid of him."

"I am. I won't be happy until he leaves Quake City, hopefully for good."

With a much lighter heart, she searched for and found Mathew in their quarters, just in time to answer Jessica's demands while Mathew readied the children for bed. Later she would bring him up to date on today's events. Though too late for his approval, she hoped he'd be pleased with how she'd handled things. A timid knock sounded and when she opened it she found her mother standing there, wringing her hands.

"Can I put the children to bed?" Eleanor said.

"No, Mother, not tonight. Sorry, see you in the morning," she said. She shut the door, wishing it had a locking mechanism and hoping her mother would leave and not stand outside like an abandoned child as she had done one previous evening. If Mother didn't want to cuddle Jessica, then she couldn't monopolise Caleb and Vanily.

Perhaps she was becoming callous and hard toward her mother, she thought. Or perhaps she was just plain tired and wanted her family to herself. By the time the children settled and Jessica went back to sleep, Calista had crawled into bed beside Mathew. His gentle snores told of his exhaustion. In the still of the night the jingle of a bridle being removed echoed from the stables across the courtyard, and the soft neighs as Bess and Buster exchanged greetings lulled her. She lay plotting tomorrow's schedule at the clinic and wondering about Peter and Daphne, who seemed to be spending a lot of time with each other and kept exchanging quick glances as if they shared a secret. Perhaps they did.

She hoped Mathew had some energy left because she intended to wake him later for a cuddle and a talk when Jessica woke for a feed, unless the baby decided to sleep through the night for the first time ever. What bliss that would be.

Three nights later she again refused Eleanor's request to put the children to bed. For as long as Eleanor continued to ignore Jessica, Calista would occasionally deny her mother access to Caleb and Vanily. It was as if the baby was invisible. It hurt more as each day passed but her mother seemed oblivious to the pain she was causing. This, coupled with the muttered complaints of the Carbonites that their sleep was being disturbed with her nightly wanderings, meant soon they'd need to get Dr Webb involved. She'd tried a herbal mix but Eleanor had spat the tea out and made a fresh one, complaining the drink was tainted with something bad.

Jessica's restlessness in the dark of night finally dragged Calista from a deep sleep and she pulled the infant from her cot beside the bed and offered her a breast. After she'd tucked the child back down she decided to check on Caleb and Vanily. The nights were cooling and the children often kicked off their covers, then woke with the early morning chill.

In the dark, she felt for their limbs and when she couldn't find them she turned on the light. To her horror, both beds were empty. She hurried out onto the landing, calling softly, wondering if they had decided to wander—or perhaps sleepwalk? No, neither had done that before. Heart pounding, fear rising in her throat, she ran down the stairs and into the kitchen. No children there. Next, she hurried along the passage to her mother's room. This is where they'd be, snuggled into bed with Grandma. But when she opened the door and saw Eleanor's bed empty as well she thought her heart would stop. Careless now of making a noise, she ran up the stairs shouting, "Mathew, Mathew. The children are gone. Mother's gone too. I think she's taken them."

By the time she'd shaken Mathew awake and they'd both stumbled back onto the landing, wearing coats and something on their feet, other doors had opened and William, Winston, Kyle and Benjamin were also ready to search. The Carbonites each volunteered to search an area within the premises before joining them outside.

Calista stood with Mathew outside the high stockade gates, her throat aching. Tears ran down her cheeks and she licked them from her lips, tasting the salt. Which way to go?

"We'll find them," Mathew said, his arm around her shoulders. "They can't be far."

"They could be anywhere. They might have been gone for hours."

Guilt swamped her and she sobbed. The thought that her mother had conspired with Wallace Howe and taken her children, stolen them away in the dead of night, caused a wail of agony to escape her throat.

In this city of crumbling buildings and places to hide, where would she find them? Or worse still, perhaps even now they were miles away in Howe's wagon, locked in the shed on the back.

Chapter 14

The chill in the air matched the ice in her heart as she watched the men scatter in various directions. Without any comment from her, they had arrived outside with solar torches and lit firebrands to aid their search, the directions each would take already decided. This left her and Mathew standing as if rooted to the spot, unsure which way they should go.

"We need to be practical here, darling." Mathew hugged her close. "Let's consider your mother's mind and ignore the possibility Howe has the children. She doesn't have a watch so how could she set a time to meet him? And if they did meet up, we can't catch up on foot. So, let's focus on the other option: that your mother has run away with them, on foot. Then there's her agoraphobia to consider, which might become worse if she's stressed, which I imagine she will be after kidnapping her grandchildren. Regardless of how happy she is wandering around in the dark, they won't be… Especially Vanily."

Calista nodded and looked into his face, barely visible in the cold, pre-dawn light. His reasoning made sense. "Yes, I imagine however brave Mother may have been to start with, it won't last long."

"So let's search nearby. We can go round all the buildings, looking in doorways and any outside sheds. I can't imagine her abandoning the children. If she had the desire to hide, she would take them with her."

"We can't go far away because one of the men might come back with the children and we won't be here." This seemed an illogical reason to stay by the gates, even as she said it, but her mind didn't seem to be functioning properly.

"They will be fine if they find the children. Those men are all like uncles to them, so don't worry about not being here at the gates." Mathew took her hand and pulled her a few steps. "First we'll check around the clinic, out the back and in the shed where the doctor keeps his trap, then we'll move on to the next house. At least we are doing something." And he tugged her further away from the gates, determined to get her moving, for she wasn't thinking straight, and her body seemed frozen with the shock of losing the children.

He was right. They had to look close to home. How could her mother do this? What motive did she have? If Howe wasn't involved nothing made sense, but with the Carbonites searching further afield this was the only option left. She followed Mathew, one hand clinging to his coat as he called softly and they looked into every nook and cranny around the neighbouring houses before moving on.

Wallace Howe wondered if his head would burst. Not used to drinking, let alone for hours on end, he'd staggered up the stairs of the boarding house and fallen on his bed, fully clad, boots on and his head spinning. Oblivion wrapped him in its gentle embrace and although his own snores disturbed him from time to time, mostly he slept. How long he'd been asleep was irrelevant when a firm grip on his shoulder shook him awake.

"Wake up, Mr Howe. We've questions for you."

He struggled to sit up, fell back and peered through the darkness. "Who are you? What do you want?" Then the realisation that someone was in his room hit him. "And get out of my room." Rage sat him upright and he swung his arms, hoping to connect with whoever had intruded his space.

"Nope." The voice said. "Not until you tell us where Eleanor and the children are, then we might leave, but it's doubtful. We're not very happy with you, Wallace."

A torch beam scanned the room, ran over his boot-clad feet, up his legs and landed in his face, blinding him. He shook his head in disbelief. Nothing like this had ever happened to him before. Was it a dream? Perhaps he was hallucinating. "Who the bloody hell are you?" he shouted into the dark, reaching toward the torch, its beam now shifted to the floor where his feet rested.

"Kyle and Winston at your service. Carbonites, both of us, and we are prepared to use violence if need be to get to the truth. Where are the children? What have you and Eleanor got planned, because we doubt she could do this on her own."

His assailant pushed his grasping hands away, then gripped his shirt front and hauled him upright. Vertigo, or the remains of his overindulgence in the devil's drink, made him sway. A second intruder held him upright.

"My you are a mess," the second voice commented. "Been on the booze?"

Wallace would have nodded if his head had co-operated, but he managed a soft "Yes."

"Where are the children," a voice hissed in his ear, "before we resort to violence."

Their questions registered at last. Eleanor and his children must be missing. Dread of something awful happening to his children made him come to his senses. "I don't know where they are. They should be at the stockade. What's happened? Are they missing? What's Eleanor got to do with it? Is she missing too?" A match flicked and the candle by his bed flared and settled. In its glow he recognised Winston and Kyle. "Are you serious?"

"We are, and you're the main suspect. We reckon you have them hidden somewhere and are waiting for dawn to spirit them away, along with their grandmother."

Wallace shook his head, "No. I agreed to leave them with their mother, with Calista. I've made no plans with Eleanor. She's too unstable to plot anything with. Believe me, I spent weeks with her, I know."

"We thought you might deny it. Just so you know, we checked the stable and your horse and wagon are still there, so you won't be using that to take them away. We're going to make sure of that."

"But I've sold them. That's why I've been drinking. The man who bought them insisted we drink to seal the contract. I don't own them anymore." He patted his top pocket; the money was still there. At least he hadn't been robbed—yet.

"Sorry, Mr Howe," said Kyle, "but you'll be coming with us. One sure way of stopping your plan is to keep you company, until you decide to tell us where they are. 'Course, you could always do that now, and then we'll leave you alone once we find them."

"I don't know where they are." How could he convince these two he was telling the truth? His throat tightened and his voice rose. "I'll even come and look for them with you."

"And lead us in the wrong direction. A likely story," Winston muttered, and proceeded to tie Wallace's hands together. They stood him on his feet once more and this time he didn't sway. The pure shock of the assault seemed to be sobering him up, but it didn't help his pounding head.

One of them blew out the candle and the smell of the smouldering wick followed them out the door. With the two men guiding him he navigated his way down the stairs and out into the road. In the murkiness the occasional light glowed, so he guessed he hadn't slept for long. It must still be the middle of the night.

"Right-oh, let's get going," Winston said, far too cheerful for this time of the night, and they set off walking at a good pace, Winston in front holding onto the rope that bound Wallace's hands and Kyle behind him. Every now and again, accidentally on purpose, Kyle would tap his ankles and he'd land on the ground. Wallace presumed this was the Carbonite version of violence because they had the reputation of being non-violent. Technically they weren't beating him up, the ground was and he continued to tell them, each time he fell, that he had no damned idea where Eleanor was—and did they truly think he'd do anything to harm his precious children?

"I love my kids," he gasped through dust-caked lips. He doubted he'd ever drink again and hoped he'd wake up from this nightmare. After what seemed a long time, he was shoved through the small door in the stockade gates and hustled across the yard into the stables. The horses woke and called to the men, who, after pushing him into a pile of hay, checked their charges with the love and concern that Wallace at that moment wished someone would show him.

"Here's a saddle blanket to keep the hay out of your hair," Kyle said, tossing a rug at him. "Are you sure you wouldn't like to tell us where the children are?"

Wallace shook his head. How many times did he have to say he didn't know?

"Right. See you in the morning," Kyle added, and joined Winston, who was waiting at the stable's door.

Once they were gone, the horses settled and Wallace slumped into the nearest pile of hay, arranged the blanket under his head and surrendered to the exhaustion that wrapped around him like a shroud. A rooster crowed nearby and chickens clucked. Must be near dawn. At least he was with the horses. It could be worse. They might have put him in the hen house.

Calista and Mathew agreed, it seemed they'd been searching for hours. In the vicinity of the stockade and clinic they'd found no trace of Eleanor or the children. Now they were walking surrounding streets, calling the children's names. Mathew had turned the torch off to conserve its battery and they seemed to be floundering in an indigo soup. They were three streets away from the stockade and Calista was losing hope when she heard a faint cry, a wail of despair, a protest even.

"Is that Vanily?"

"Maybe, or another child in distress." They stood listening to the autumn chorus of crickets calling their last mating calls before winter made them burrow into the earth. A morepork called in the distance and another answered nearby. They were about to move off, hope abandoned, when they heard the cry again.

"Sounds like her," said Mathew, and he hurried on, calling, "Caleb, Vanily, where are you? Daddy's here." Again a thin howl pierced the dark and they turned toward it, down an alleyway between two houses, following the thin sound. A third cry broke, clipped short with a muffled ending and Calista's stomach roiled. It sounded like Vanily, but it could be any small child. Was she building a false hope? They stopped again, silent, listening, not sure where the sound had come from this time, prepared to backtrack if they had to—and then Mathew bellowed, "Caleb, it's Daddy and Mummy. We're looking for you. This is not a game."

"Daaaaddy." Again the high pitched cry split the air, followed by Caleb's voice shouting "Oh, Vanily, you've spoiled the game. Now Grandma will be even crosser."

The voice seemed to be coming from over the fence and feeling their way along looking for a way in, they found an opening. Several missing boards allowed them to duck into the back yard of a house. They stopped again, hoping for confirmation they were heading in the right direction. In the pitch blackness of the yard, Calista saw a faint glow in the distance, a beautiful green glow, shimmering, disappearing and bobbing into view again. Someone with Angel's Kiss was in the yard. It could be Mother. She'd displayed the symptoms at the community meeting, just before they left the tunnels. Sometimes she wondered if the sickness had spread to her mother's mind. A tug on Mathew's arm drew his attention to where she was pointing. "There, look over there."

"I see it."

"Whoever it is, the poor creature has Angel's Kiss. We have to go to them. They might have seen the children." Her words split the darkness and they stumbled through the long grass, which wrapped around their ankles like damp string. The glow grew brighter as they approached.

Sobs broke the dark, coming from the same place, and the weak light of their torch revealed a small shelter in the corner of the garden. In it huddled Eleanor, against the stack of wood, her frail body and her head with its glowing hair pressed into a corner like a frightened bird. Sitting beside her on a pile of split logs were the children, clad only in their nightclothes, shivering, with Caleb holding Vanily's hand and Vanily shuddering between suppressed sobs.

Ignoring her mother for the moment and careful not to show too much emotion, Calista knelt beside them and whispered. "What are you doing out here in the dark?" Vanily slipped off her perch and climbed onto Mathew's lap as he knelt beside Calista, but Caleb sat tall, looking very grownup for a six-year-old, and began his story.

"I'm taking Grandma to see Angela. I know the way, even in the dark, but Grandma got frightened. And then we found this shed and now she won't move. I keep telling her Angela will give us a drink and even a nice warm bed, but she won't move, Mummy. I told Grandma Vanily was too small to come with us, but Grandma said she would be fine. I was right, Mummy. Vanily keeps crying and spoiling the game."

"What game?" Mathew said. Calista could see him stroking Vanily's blond curls.

"We're playing hide and seek, just for a little while until Grandma feels better. Grandma said she wants to surprise Granddad and Angela. Mr Howe told her about Angela. He said it was a secret but I said Angela wasn't a secret. Everybody knows Angela. Angela is lovely. Everyone says so. I told her about Colin and Belinda and their house where Granddad stays." He sniffed. Indignation coloured his voice. "She didn't believe me, Mummy. Grandma said she had to see for herself, so I'm taking her there."

Calista ruffled his hair and kissed her small son's cheek. He'd experienced so much in the past year and was, in all circumstances, always honest. "Never mind, love, we believe you."

"Silly game, silly Grandma," Vanily murmured, and then buried her face into Mathew's coat.

Calista looked at Eleanor, who'd turned around to face them. The torchlight dimmed the glow of her radiation sickness but the set of Eleanor's jaw told Calista she was in for a tongue-lashing.

She reached to help her mother up. "Come on, Mother, you're ill. Let's get you home. You must be in pain. Dr Webb will be able to give you something to help you rest."

Eleanor batted her hand away. "You lied." she hissed. "You lied to me. How dare you lie to your mother, after all I've done for you!" Her eyes flashed in the torchlight and she struggled to stand, but couldn't.

"I didn't lie, Mother, I simply avoided telling you—and so did everyone else. If anyone is to blame, it's Father's fault. He's the one you should be mad at, not me. I didn't know for ages and only found out by accident when we were in Cheviot. No one wanted to tell me that Father had another wife and another family. I know how you feel. I've experienced it, but you need to discuss it with him." She reached to help her mother up, but Eleanor ducked around her at a crouch and then stood.

"Sort things out? How?" she screeched. "Now I'm married to a bigamist. After all the sacrifices I made for the damned Carbonites and his dreams of freedom. Damn the man!" and she ran, bent over, stumbling across the garden, through the gap in the fence and disappeared.

Calista made to follow but Mathew held her arm. "Leave her be, honey, there's little we can do. She'll find her way back or someone will find her. It'll be easier in the daylight. Everyone knows she's Aaron's wife and lives with us. It's common knowledge around the city." He helped her to her feet. "We have to get these children home."

"Grandma has a map," said Caleb. "I drew it for her. She'll be able to find her way to Granddad's when the sun comes up. I'm a good drawer." Caleb clutched her hand. "Remember, Mummy? I showed you the map."

And he had, just a few days before, when he'd drawn the gates of the stockade with a X beside them, the double-storied house on the corner where the Fletchers lived, and then two sheep in a paddock, and a cat sitting on a post where Mrs Govern lived. Lower down the page he'd drawn a crucifix for the tumbled-down church and a lot of wriggly lines for the river running beside it. Finally he'd drawn another X for his grandfather's house. She'd admired it but had never thought why he might be making a map. Now she knew.

"Mathew, the others will still be looking," Calista realised, as she guided Caleb through the hole in the fence.

"It's okay, I pressed my pendant. They'll know we've found them." He helped Vanily through the gap and lifted her onto his hip. They each took one of Caleb's hands and swung him off the ground, a thing he loved them to do.

"Time to go home and back to bed," Mathew softly sang each time they lifted him, until their arms ached, and they ceased the game.

Their journey back was in a straighter line than their outward search but equally slow as Caleb kept stopping, looking behind for his grandmother. Despite his questions, Calista couldn't find the words to explain bigamy or why Grandma was so angry and had run away.

"I told Grandma Angela is lovely. I told her what good fun Colin and Belinda are. Why has she run away, Mummy?"

"One day when you are grown up, I'll explain it to you, Caleb. It's just a bit complicated for a small boy to understand. Isn't it, Mathew?" and Mathew agreed and promised to take them for a wagon ride in the morning. They could miss school and daycare and have a day out with him.

Dawn was splitting the clouds with bars of light by the time they turned into their street. The stockade gates were just visible in the distance and as they neared the clinic the door opened and Mary came out, soft-footing her way down the steps and hurrying ahead of them. She hadn't seen them.

Calista giggled and caught Mathew's gaze. "No wonder Mary didn't stir when we all got up to search," she whispered. "She's going to be so embarrassed when she finds we are all up and now everyone knows where she spent the night."

"She may as well make it official," said Mathew. "At least we'll get another spare room if she goes to live with the doctor and Daisy."

"Why is Mary going to live with Daisy?" Caleb asked.

"More grownup stuff," said Calista. "I'll tell you when you're older."

"I's older," said Vanily, briefly taking her thumb out of her mouth. "Grandma said I's old enough to go on a 'venture."

"Quite right," said Mathew. "We'll go on an adventure in the morning."

Calista wondered what else her mother had told the children. She'd have to come home eventually, and then there'd be another confrontation. Not something to look forward to.

Calista and Mathew headed for the kitchen after putting the children to bed. The men were already gathered around the table, swapping their middle-of-the-night tales of what they'd seen and where they'd been in the search. Many of the things they saw were cause for amusement, including catching Mary coming home. Poor Mary had given up blushing and was now giving them as much cheek as she'd received.

They all turned when the front door slammed, expecting Eleanor, but it was Cyril who came in.

"An early morning party and I wasn't invited," he said.

"And where have you been? Out carousing?" Mary quipped.

"No, I've been celebrating. Tying up the deal I made with Wallace Howe. I bought his horse and wagon and I'm taking him to Timaru tomorrow. He can find his way home from there." There was an exchange of glances. "What?" Cyril said. "What have I missed?"

"So you've been with Howe, all night?" Benjamin said.

Cyril nodded, "Most of it. I had to walk him to his boarding house. He's not a drinker, I discovered. Since then I've had two hours sleep. Why? Have I missed something?"

"Just the search for two abducted children who are now safe, but Eleanor is still missing," said Kyle. "At least we know that Howe wasn't involved, because he was our prime enabler, until a moment ago."

"You can cross him off your list. I can vouch for his innocence, at least during the night, plus I'm taking him away tomorrow. You mightn't ever see him again."

"Oh, we'll see him again alright," Winston said with a wry smile, "because we have him over in the stables, hands tied so he can't escape. He's sleeping in the hay."

Over the general amusement, Cyril said, "That's hardly the right way to treat my first customer. I'd better go and get him." He looked at Mary. "Make him a cup of tea and some breakfast, please, Mary. The poor man must be dying of thirst."

"I'll get my bike and cycle to Master Aaron's," said Kyle. "He'll have to know his wife is missing." He looked at Calista and Mathew. "Better head to bed, you two, it's going to be a long day of searching for Eleanor for the rest of us."

Chapter 15

Was that a knock on the front door? Angela stopped peeling the vegetables for dinner and listened. There it was again, soft and almost apologetic. She wiped her hands on her apron and hurried into the passageway, well used to people coming to the door, but usually they thundered their request to be admitted.

She opened the door. "Yes?" she said, "Can I help you?"

A frail woman stood on the porch, dishevelled, with bits of grass in her hair, almost tramp-like except for her fine cotton nightwear and the soft leather slippers on her feet.

"Is Aaron in? Does he live here?" The lady's gaze flitted sideways as if she was being pursued. Then, as if the thought had just occurred to her, she added, "I want to see him", and she stood on tiptoe looking over Angela's shoulder.

This must be Eleanor, Aaron's wife, who'd taken the children out of their beds last night, causing most of the Carbonites to be out for hours searching. Except for Aaron, who'd heard about it at dawn and was this minute hunting for her as well. Somehow, she had to keep her here until Aaron returned.

"You look quite tired and dusty," Angela said, and opened the door wider. "Can I get you a nice cup of tea, or something to eat? I've just made some biscuits. Aaron should be back soon."

The woman turned and for a moment Angela thought she would bolt down the path and leave, but instead, she turned back and nodded. "That would be very nice, thank you. I've had a long walk to get here and I could do with something to drink."

"Come in, come in." Angela waved her through the door and pointed down the hall. "The kitchen is the second door on the left, just go in and take a seat, unless you'd like to wash your hands?"

"I'd like that," the woman said. "I'm a bit of a mess. Can't meet Aaron like this."

Angela guided her to the bathroom and slipped back to latch the front door, but the woman didn't leave, she came into the kitchen and sat on a chair at the table, giving a deep sigh. Angela busied herself making them both a cup of tea, searching for a way to make her visitor comfortable and perhaps get her to confirm her identity. How she wished Aaron was here. The clock chimed three o'clock from the hall. "The children will be home from school soon. Do you have children or grandchildren?" The woman nodded but didn't speak. "I'm called Angela, what's your name?"

Would she tell her? Angela waited, putting the cup in front of her visitor and sliding a plate of biscuits across the table.

"You can call me Ellie," the woman said. "No one has called me that since my parents died."

"Was that long ago?"

"Many years. They were part of the original settlers in the tunnels. Mother told me they were so excited to win a place on the ballot. So wonderful to be able to live in safety, away from the radiation that was approaching New Zealand as it circled the globe from Europe and the United States."

"Do you remember going into the tunnels?" Angela decided this was a safe topic to extend.

"No, I was born in the tunnels. I've just recently come out. I'm finding it all very strange. I think everyone was tricked. It was all a lie. The radiation is everywhere, and we weren't safe at all."

Knowing the story, Angela thought about her next question, then took the plunge. "I hear the recent earthquakes were very destructive. You obviously survived them. Were you somewhere safe when they struck?"

Eleanor shuddered and for a moment Angela thought she'd lost her attention as Eleanor's expression became vacant, almost deranged, as her lips pulled back to reveal yellowed teeth. Perhaps she'd misjudged her approach, and then Eleanor stirred her cup for a moment and looked up, meeting Angela's gaze, her face now calm.

"No, I was in the middle of it. It was awful. People were crushed under the rock ceiling of the dining room. There were screams and moans and you could smell the terror in the air. We ran in all directions, finding passages blocked, using side doors and service passages, always heading south until we found the railway line. We followed that." She moaned and put her head in her hands.

Angela stood and moved around the table to touch Eleanor's shoulder, rubbing her back and stroking her hair. "How dreadful for you. I'm so sorry talking about it has triggered bad memories. It's amazing you survived."

She pushed a handkerchief into Eleanor's hand, and waited until she'd stopped sniffling and wiped her face. "We walked for days down those tracks, through water, mud and human remains. My feet were in ribbons by the time we got out and I think my mind was cut to pieces too. It's never been the same since."

"But you lived. Well done, such a miracle," Angela said, putting a positive spin on her comments, hoping to prevent more tears.

"No one else has asked me about how I escaped. I didn't think people cared."

"Perhaps people just don't know what to say and don't want to upset you," Angela said, and refilled the plate of biscuits, which Eleanor had managed to clear between her tears and telling her story. Her hunger was evident yet restrained.

If only she could get hold of Aaron, but she didn't have a pendant and Colin was too young to send to the stockade when he came home from school.

"You have a nice house here," Eleanor said, her gaze scanning the room.

Angela looked at the polished rimu floors with the scattered rag rugs she'd made. The sun poured in the bay window and the daisies in the small vase on the table looked lovely. Belinda had picked them yesterday for her. The coal stove gleamed, making the old electric stove beside it look like a poor relation. "Yes, it's a lovely old home. Spacious and well insulated. We were lucky to get it. Aaron found a coal range and we fixed up the chimney. It's great when the electricity supply fails. The house has good bones, as they say, and it's swayed its way through a lot of earthquakes. Only the chimney cracks when we get a good shake." The conversation was bordering on the ridiculous. Eleanor, sitting there pretending to be someone else, and here she was going along with the farce.

"Are you married to Aaron?" Eleanor asked, and shivered.

Hoping to avoid the question, Angela said, "You're cold; let me get you something warm." She ducked out into the hallway and brought back a red-and-black check jacket which she eased onto Eleanor, making her put her arms in the sleeves.

Then Eleanor asked again, "Are you married?"

"No, Aaron has a wife, in the tunnels." She couldn't resist adding, "You may know her."

Eleanor shook her head. "I don't know many people and lots have died. No one lives there anymore."

The charade continued. "Aaron told me he was married the first time I met him. He's a kind man. Always worrying about other people, and he often brings someone home for a meal and then finds them shelter. He's a wonderful father to our children." She paused, but Eleanor didn't speak so she continued, "He's a husband to me in every respect, except for a piece of paper in the Court records." Fed up with this game, she asked, "What do you want to see him about?"

"I need to talk to him. There are things I need to say," and Eleanor's lips formed a tight line.

Angela refreshed the teapot and then fussed about at the bench, cutting more vegetables for the stew, leaving Eleanor to her thoughts and more tea.

The flyscreen door banged on the back porch and high voices sounded, followed by a deep rumble of laughter. Aaron was home. He must have collected the children from school. This would be interesting. The clatter of small feet echoed up the passage and the roar of an imaginary lion followed them as the children ran into the room and hid behind Angela. Aaron pounced over the threshold, arms outstretched, fingers clawed, growling like a monster. The children giggled. Aaron stopped mid-stride, stood upright, dropped his arms and gaped.

"Eleanor?" He stepped closer and smiled. "Eleanor, thank God you're safe. We've been searching the city for you." He looked at Angela, eyebrows raised, and she shrugged.

She had no idea where this discussion should go but she knew it wasn't her place to participate. She grabbed biscuits from the table and gathered the children in front of her. "We'll go and feed the chickens and get the eggs," she said and led Colin and Belinda out of the room, silencing their queries about their visitor with a sharp shake of her head.

Aaron pulled up a chair close to Eleanor, put his arm across her shoulder and kissed her cheek. "What have you been up to, Lovey?"

She locked her gaze on his and fingered his beard, now a lot tidier than it had been on his visits to the tunnels over the years. "I have lots to say and I'd like you to listen without arguing." He nodded. "I've been very angry for the past few days. So angry I dragged Caleb and Vanily out of their beds for a midnight tramp. I wanted to find you, to shout at you, to ask why you created another family while I stayed in the dark in the tunnels."

He sat back and said, "But you wouldn't leave. I begged you, time and again, Eleanor. I gave up asking in the end. Every time I returned and the MICs threw me out I asked you to come with me. You refused to budge. I should have told you about Angela, but the time never seemed right."

"Yes, you should have told me. It wasn't nice to hear it from Wallace Howe. He looked so smug and I wanted to kick his shins." She twisted her hands in her lap, and he waited, remembering her request that he didn't argue. She took a deep breath and continued. "I want to tell you I was wrong. I believed all the lies they told. I know now that there's as much radiation in the tunnels as there is outside."

"You weren't the only one fooled. Many have died still believing that."

"But I'm not angry anymore." She grasped his hand. "Rage drove me to do stupid things, but it's gone. Now I'm just tired and sad. Caleb was right. Angela is lovely. You made a good choice and I think your children are beautiful. If Caleb loves them they must be good kids, and Belinda looks so much like Calista as a child, except she has more curls. Don't you think?"

"She does. I've always thought that," he said.

They both smiled at the memory and then Eleanor stood. "I'm going to leave now. I've seen your family and where you live. It's a lovely old wooden house. You will be safe here. I'm going back to the stockade now. I don't know what I'm going to do with the rest of my life, but you can have a divorce if you want one."

He stood and reached for her, but she stepped back. "No, Aaron. I don't want your love any longer. You need to give it to your new family."

"I have enough love for two women. I've always loved you, I've never stopped." He followed her to the door. "Let me walk you back. Calista is distraught."

"No. I have Caleb's map. I'll turn it up the other way and follow it again. On the way here, when I reached the broken church everyone I asked knew where you lived. I'm sure people will tell me the way to the stockade if I get lost."

"But what about…?"

"If the terror comes back I'll just hide until it passes." She stiffened her back. "I have to do this. I have to learn to be outside. I'm getting better and it's easier now that I'm not so angry." She swallowed hard and he guessed she was fighting her fear.

He led her to the front door and again grasped her arm. "Please let me take you back."

She swatted his hand away, as you would a child's questing fingers. "Leave me be. My brain is sometimes covered with a blanket of fog and then a corner lifts and I can think clearly. Let me make the most of this clear time, please. Some days I feel quite weak, but I'm feeling strong today."

"Calista thinks you are not well."

"I know, I heard her in the night. She thinks I have Angel's Kiss, such a lovely name for a horrible thing." She sighed and stepped out onto the front porch, then turned and quickly kissed him, a mere brush of her lips on his. "You're a good man, Aaron, just as Angela says. You have too much heart to be sensible at times, but that's a good fault." She walked down the path and raised her hand in a small wave after she shut the gate, a strange sight in her long nightwear and Angela's checked jacket over the top. At least she'd be warm on her way home.

His heart tightened and his stomach clenched. Regret swamped him. He could have handled that better. But would rehashing old memories have helped? Probably not, better to move on. He wandered outside to find his family; he hugged his children and kissed Angela, grateful for Eleanor's forgiveness.

A loud hammering on the back door dragged Aaron from sleep, and he slipped out of bed and hurried to answer before the pounding woke Angela and the children. At this time of night, it could only be a disaster of some kind. People didn't wander around the unlit streets without good reason.

He lifted the stick from beside the door and with it behind one leg he opened the door until the snag chain stopped it, and then peered through the gap. "Yes? What is it?"

"Mr Waterman?"

"That's me."

"Sir, I have bad news. My name is Constable Higgins from the Ferrymead Police. A body has been found in the estuary behind Brighton Beach."

Aaron's heart lurched. For five days they had been searching for Eleanor. She'd never arrived at the stockade. He'd asked everyone he knew to look for her and his followers had also spread the word. Could it be her?

"And you think it's my wife?" He undid the chain and opened the door. In the light of the dim electric bulb in the hallway, the constable stood, a picture of sadness, as if he'd practised being the bearer of bad news. His hands clutched his police issue hat, its reflector band glowing, confirming his status.

"We do, sir. And if you could come with me we'd like you to view the body. It may be some other poor soul, but it is a female and she's wearing a nightgown, a jacket and one shoe. Not the usual attire to go swimming. The medical officer will do a postmortem but his initial opinion is that the lady drowned."

Aaron couldn't move. His bare feet seemed glued to the floor while his emotions cascaded through him: grief for his wife, relief that she was no longer a problem, and then a wave of guilt that he could even think that way. She must have stumbled and fallen into the river in the dark. She'd have floundered immediately. No one reared in the tunnels knew how to swim.

"Come in," he gestured, and shut the door behind the constable. "I'll get some clothes on and be back in a moment." He tiptoed back into the bedroom and to Angela's mumbled query said, "It's nothing, just go back to sleep. I have to go out for a few hours. I'll be back by breakfast time, I hope."

Together they walked to the police station, no small distance but at least he felt safe walking beside the policeman. He was hardly likely to be mugged with the constable for company, the pale moon lighting the reflecting tape on the constable's hat and shoulder pads.

"Couldn't this have waited until morning?" he wondered aloud.

"Surely it's not an emergency if the poor lady is dead?"

"True," Constable Higgins said, "but we have a heavy workload and lots of thievery to solve. Identification of bodies is not a priority unless it's a murder, but in this instant, I'd heard the rumours of your wife's disappearance and I felt sure you would want to know."

"Very kind of you," Aaron said.

"Besides, the Carbonites have been very good to my sister and I wanted to do something in return, so I volunteered to be the one to tell you."

"A fine sentiment, indeed, thank you," and Aaron wondered which of the women they'd helped was related to the constable. Not that it mattered. There were so many women alone, it made his heart ache, and as William once said he "couldn't marry all of them", a sly dig at Aaron's bigamist status. Sometimes the heart has a mind of its own and in Angela's case, he'd been smitten and lost within days of meeting her.

If the body was indeed Eleanor then he'd need to arrange a funeral and burial. Where could he put her that would make her happy? She hated the outdoors, but he could hardly bury her inside. His stomach clenched as he thought of Calista and her reaction to losing her mother. She'd already squarely laid the blame for Eleanor's disappearance at his feet, insisting he should have told Eleanor of his relationship with Angela. According to his daughter, he'd put his grandchildren at risk as well. A man couldn't win when a woman set against him—not to mention that conniving Howe.

While Caleb insisted Wallace Howe had told his grandmother of Angela's existence, Calista still blamed him. Thank Heavens the damned man had left along with Cyril, who'd promised Aaron he would ensure Howe reached Timaru and found onward transport. Howe had cost him most of his savings, demanding compensation, whinging about the wagon modification to bring Eleanor north, moaning about the cost in time and money. Then, once Aaron had paid him one hundred kiwis, Howe had switched tack and tried to make out he'd done it from the goodness of his heart.

Pure rubbish, all the man wanted was access to Caleb and Vanily. While Calista's strong will at times annoyed him, at least she'd put Howe in his place regarding his claims on the children.

The pale blue light on the police station's roof glowed in the distance and he lengthened his stride. Time to find out if his wife was dead or whether it was some other poor soul.

The morgue masqueraded as a concrete shed at the rear of the station, cold enough to double as a cooler, even in summer. Now, in the autumn dawn, he shivered as he watched the constable gently fold back the sheet. Yes, it was her. Her long dark hair, now threaded with grey and holding bits of sand and driftwood, lay over her shoulder. Her thin arms had been crossed over her chest and he caressed her cold, stiff hands. He leaned and kissed her icy lips, remembering the heat of their young passion and the warmth of her love, all gone forever.

Even when she'd arrived in Quake City, the experience of surviving the earthquake had corrupted her ability to love. All that remained had been her ties to Caleb and Vanily. How she must have suffered in those days immediately after the quake. No one would ever know what she went through. She lay as rigid now as she had been each time he'd tried to hold her in the past few weeks, desperate to reconnect, trying to rekindle her spark for life, wanting to share memories; his attempts to communicate met time and again with a frost-laden stare.

"Yes, it is my wife, Eleanor Waterman. I'm happy to sign a statement to that effect."

Constable Higgins laid his hand on Aaron's shoulder and squeezed, no doubt meaning it to be an act of comfort. Aaron resisted the urge to swipe his hand away. Like an animal in pain, he wanted to crawl away somewhere dark and leave the world to go on without him.

He shook his head, commanding himself to get real and be practical. There were things to do: papers to sign, arrangements to be made, a daughter to tell and good works to carry on with. Death didn't stop the world, even if you wanted it to.

"May I?" He pointed to the gold band on Eleanor's left hand. It would be nice to give it to Calista. Gold rings were precious and he wondered why it hadn't been stolen. There were honest people in the world after all. The young couple who'd found her had not been able to afford a ring, and his daughter would treasure it as part of her mother's heritage. He sought comfort from this as he worked the ring over Eleanor's knuckle and slipped it into his pocket, before covering his wife's face and walking away, as he'd done so many times in the past.

Chapter 16

The sound of Pelly's feet hurrying down the passage caused Calista to lift her head and watch to see if it was her door, or Dr Webb's, that would be thrown open. The girl had never learned to walk calmly or quietly in cases of urgency. The click of heels stopped outside; it was her turn to receive Pelly's breathless news. In what Calista decided was an effort to meet the desired state of decorum, the doorknob slowly revolved, then Pelly opened her office door and stepped sedately in.

"An emergency?" Calista asked, raising her eyebrows and smiling at the beaming face. The young lady never seemed daunted by any of life's problems. even though she thundered down the hall to announce incoming news. Her ready smile and willingness to help made her a favourite amongst their clients and although she refused to work at the crèche, or even help Daphne part-time, Pelly often had a baby on her hip while the parent consulted with the doctor, or a young child would be found sitting on a high stool at the reception desk, earnestly colouring in an animal that Pelly had drawn.

"Sorry to interrupt, but there's a lady at the desk. She's tied her horse up outside on the hitching rail"—Pelly took a huge breath—"and she says to tell you her name is Doctor Elizabeth and she's come to see you. Is she a real doctor? Do you know her? She's short and doesn't look strong enough to be a doctor."

"She certainly is a doctor, and yes, please, tell her I'll be there in a minute."

Elizabeth? Here? Calista had last seen her high above the town of Cheviot, where they'd parted ways, Elizabeth to head north on her travels and Calista to return to the boarding house and Mathew. How long ago? Nearly two years? So much had happened since.

Her thoughts skittered as she gathered up the accounts and correspondence she'd been working on and slipped them into their folders, tossed them into a drawer in her desk, and shut her office door behind her. No more work today, only joyful conversation with the woman she considered to be the nearest thing she had to a best friend.

And there she was, looking a little older, a few more lines around her eyes, but tanned and beaming a welcome. Elizabeth's hair hung in a long, dark plait over her shoulder, wispy bits poking out here and there, and around her hairline a few strands curled. She seemed smaller than Calista remembered, probably because Pelly was quite tall, but she looked as lovely as ever. Her gaze held Calista's, her eyes brown and warm, her smile like sunshine on a rainy day.

"Oh, Elizabeth!" She ran into Elizabeth's widespread arms and they hugged each other tight for long seconds that stretched on and on, until Pelly coughed and said, "Looks like you know each other." This made them release their hug and Calista turned and introduced Elizabeth to Pelly.

"This is our receptionist, Pelly, without whom we'd all be completely lost. Pelly, this is my dear friend, Dr Elizabeth Falwasser."

"Dr Elizabeth is just fine."

Calista took Elizabeth's hand, not wanting to share a moment of Elizabeth's time and attention with anyone and led her to the door. "I'm off for the day, Pelly," she said over her shoulder, as they went out.

"Pelly said you have a horse? You said you'd never get a horse. You turned down the one that injured boy's father offered you when we were staying at the Pendergast's place."

"I know, but on the way back I stopped there, and the boy and Harold, his father, came by for a checkup. Your handiwork is still great, only a fine line of a scar. He offered me a horse once more and this time I accepted. I had so many leaves to carry. All the families in the valley had picked with me." She sighed and leaned against the pony. "Besides, I'm tired of walking and I heard about the Carbonites' stockade on my travels." She patted the horse's wither. "I'm begging a bed for the night and a stall for my horse."

She looked so tired that Calista had to resist the urge to pat her back and hug her again. Her horse had a bulging sack hanging on each side of the saddle horn and full panniers on each side of its rump. Bulky but not heavy, she decided.

"Follow me. You shall have both your wishes granted." She unhitched the horse and taking Elizabeth's hand, led them down the street to the stockade's high gates. "You can stay as many nights as you like. We have spare rooms." Both her mother's and Mary Sutton's were available, now that Mary had moved in with Dr Webb after their marriage.

She ducked through the door, opened one of the high gates, and led the horse to the stables. Benjamin was working on repairing a bridle and he agreed to feed, water and even brush the pony down while she took Elizabeth inside.

She gave Elizabeth the choice of rooms and left her to wash while she made them tea. Once they'd settled into the easy chairs in the lounge, she asked, "What have you been doing for the past two years? Where have you been? I'm so envious of you travelling the country helping people. I so want to leave here and train to be a doctor."

"You will do no such thing." Elizabeth's tone suggested she wouldn't accept disagreement. "It's exhausting. Not as rewarding as I'd hoped, and I intend to open up a small shop at the Medical School. Once I reach Dunedin, I'm going to make herbal potions and remedies and sell them." She leaned back in the chair, her cup balanced in her hands, and sighed, "I'm so tired I can't even envisage the rest of the journey south."

"Then don't go." Solutions flooded into Calista's mind and tumbled out her mouth. "Dr Webb and his wife and daughter have just moved out of the rooms behind the clinic"—she waved her hands in the direction of the clinic—"where you found me. You could live there and make your herbal remedies." She leaned forward, lifted her teacup and placed it on the saucer on the side table, then took Elizabeth's hands in hers. "I could help you. I want to help you. It would be as good as being a doctor—and you might even like to help Dr Webb sometimes, on the days he's away visiting other places. He's so overworked. Even on the days he isn't here, people queue up waiting, hoping he will return early. He never does." She squeezed Elizabeth's hands and watched her expression, hoping for a spark of interest.

"Who owns the clinic buildings? I might not be able to afford the rent."

"We do. We have barter or cash payments, so we get food and money, and it's now paying its way. I don't think my father will charge you if you are helping the people. The Carbonites built the clinic for Dr Webb to use. He helped us escape from the tunnels and agreed to come to Quake City to set up a clinic because we promised to support him."

"But you weren't in the tunnels when I met you. You'd already left. Was Dr Webb already here? I hadn't heard that." Confusion etched lines on Elizabeth's brow.

"Oh dear, a lot has happened since Cheviot. That was nearly two years ago." She took a deep breath. "Do you truly want to know?" Elizabeth nodded. "Well, long story short, I was kidnapped when I tried to return to the stockade, from right in front of the gates; two men snatched me and carted me off to Arthur's Pass, onto the train and back to Erewhon Station community. Then a couple of months later Mathew broke into the tunnels through the air conditioning ducts to find me, and about twenty-five of us managed to escape late one night. Dr Webb came with us down the mountain in the dark."

"So you missed the earthquakes?"

"Yes, by just by a few hours. We were so lucky! By morning we'd reached the bottom where the wagons were waiting and we were out on the plains when the earthquakes struck." She paused as the memories flooded back. "It was dreadful and yet magnificently awesome. We saw the Southern Alps roll and shake. Rocks fell, snow cascaded and of course we all ended up on the ground as it rolled and threw us about."

"What luck. And your mother? I presume she came with you."

Calista's breath hitched. It always did when she thought of her mother, and she rolled the gold wedding ring around her finger. "No, at the last moment she ran back, but she managed to get out of tunnels after the quakes, with severe injuries to her feet—and her mind. It's a long story, and sad. She's no longer with us. She drowned about five months ago. She was terrified of the outdoors and had Angel's Kiss, so perhaps drowning was the kindest way to die." Salty tears rolled down the side of her nose and she caught them with her tongue as they reached her lips. "Sorry," she mumbled, wiping her eyes.

"It's perfectly natural to be upset. I'm used to seeing tears." Elizabeth leaned forward to hug her. "You poor darling. And what about your children? A boy and a girl, I remember. You brought them out of the tunnels with you?"

"Yes, Mathew is wonderful to them, and we have a new daughter, Jessica. She's nearly a year old." Calista straightened her back, sat tall and sniffed, burying all her excess emotion. She smiled. "If I hadn't been with you in the valley with the Pendergasts, getting the native foliage, I'd never have seen Angel's Kiss on that sick child. The lights went out during a community meeting in the tunnels and Elizabeth, you'd have been horrified, there were cases of Angel's Kiss everywhere among the people there." She shook her head at the memory of that night. "Everyone could see it in the dark and Dr Webb backed me up when I told them there was as much radiation in the tunnels as there was outside. The cases of Angel's Kiss proved it. A few believed me and left with us two nights later, but most of them died in the quakes, still believing they were safer inside."

"You can't make people believe things. I know. Even convincing people to try my natural remedies is hard work. Sometimes sulphur powder will work, but often they need more than that."

"We get our sulphur powder from the Medical School. It's shipped from Rotorua and we have a cartage service now that runs between Timaru and here, so it's quicker to get supplies, and more reliable than a couple of years ago."

She poured them both more tea and listened to Elizabeth's tales of her travels, her joys and her disappointments, before they set off to the crèche to collect the children, with Elizabeth promising to consider her suggestion.

"I know the Carbonites will agree. Everyone will want you to stay—and we can stable your horse. You'll be free to come and go, and to harvest more leaves."

Perhaps she could go too, but she'd leave that suggestion until later.

If only Elizabeth would say yes! They would have another doctor at the clinic, a herbal remedy dispensary, and she would be able to help Elizabeth as well as Dr Webb. She would find someone else to do the administration.

Calista hated these early mornings, with Jessica teething and fussy. It was easier to take her downstairs than wake Mathew and the children. She propped the baby on her hip and navigated the stairs, taking care not to misstep. The weak dawn light filtered through the top windows above the staircase, giving a soft patina to everything, hiding the dents in the banister and the faded carpet.

She'd just reached the bottom when the door to the guest room creaked. Josephine was staying overnight with Connor, having arrived yesterday from the farm for "a sanity break", she said. Expecting to see Josephine emerge, she walked along the passage to greet her, assuming also that Connor was awake. To her surprise, Cyril Fogarty soft-footed his way into the passage. She didn't know who was the most surprised, except his wry smile of embarrassment said it all. He'd been in Josephine's bed and was hoping to leave before the household stirred.

"Morning, Cyril," she said, not knowing what else to say.

"Morning, Calista, looks like it's going to be a lovely day," he replied, and he tip-toed past her to the front door. She watched as he carefully unlocked the door and slipped out into the pale morning.

Another twist in life! What next, she wondered? Cyril and Josephine, an unlikely match. And just what was Josephine doing having an illicit rendezvous when she was supposedly happily married? She heated some milk for the baby and sat with her in Mary's rocking chair, singing softly, hoping the child would return to sleep.

Minutes later, the kitchen door opened and Josephine came around the door's edge, a sheepish grin below her bed-tousled hair, which looked like an auburn river flowing over her shoulders.

"Did you see Cyril?" she asked.

"I did."

"You will be wondering what I'm up to."

"It's probably none of my business, except I think you are being foolish. You're putting your marriage at risk."

Josephine sat at the table alongside Calista and said, "I'm actually trying to save my marriage."

Calista raised her eyebrows and Josephine reached and held her wrist. "Let me explain."

Calista nodded. "It might take a bit of explaining. All I see is a married woman breaking her marriage vows. I know Cyril is attractive, but I would have thought you could resist his charms."

"I'll be frank," said Josephine. "I like being the squire's wife, mistress of the farm. I'm fond of Castor and despite his outward brashness, he can be kind and thoughtful. That said, he is also fixated on us having more children. Connor is now eight months old and it's not from lack of trying, but I haven't conceived." Josephine appeared to be gathering her thoughts. "I suspect my husband is infertile," she said. "For all the years of carousing before our marriage, he has never been named as the father of a child—and we both know that he is not Connor's father."

"You, me and the doctor," Calista agreed. wondering where this was heading.

"As you pointed out, Cyril is a handsome man, but more importantly he's the same colouring as my husband, the same stocky build and even taller, which is not a bad fault. I am trying to conceive a child with Cyril so that this time I have a child that resembles Castor, which Connor certainly doesn't."

"He does have your colouring, but he's very fine-boned, which you are not."

"Agreed," Josephine said. "I'm telling Castor that he is the image of my grandmother, who was a tiny lady."

"Was she?"

"I've no idea. She died when I was small, but no one else knows of her so it's a handy excuse and unable to be disproved. This time I want a child to at least have a physical resemblance to Castor."

Calista shook her head. "But you may be wrong. Perhaps Castor is fertile and it's some other reason."

"I weaned Connor several months ago, thinking feeding him may be causing me to not conceive, but that hasn't helped. I can't wait for a year or more. I need to have more children and have them close. I'm not as young as everyone thinks I am. It won't get any easier." Josephine ran her fingers through her hair, pulling her tresses off her face. "I'm doing this to save my marriage. If I don't conceive, Castor will look for a second wife. I don't want that. Then if a second wife doesn't conceive he might look on Connor with suspicion." She sighed. "See, Calista, I'm trying to keep everyone happy. We both know fertility has been affected by the radiation levels, and it's not just women it happens to, the men just don't like to admit to it."

The two of them sat in silence, Calista digesting the news. Josephine seemed to be waiting for her next question. "What about Cyril? Is he happy with this arrangement? Will you be calling on his services again?"

Josephine giggled, then pulled her face into a serious expression. "Let me say this, he's very willing to oblige, now and in the future. He won't tell, and I know you won't either."

"I seem to be the holder of your secrets and I don't enjoy it. I wish I didn't have to be."

Josephine rose and placed her hand on Calista's shoulder. "You are my friend, Calista. I need a good friend I can talk to. There is no one else I can share my secrets with, except you." She bent and kissed Calista's cheek. "I could move into a hotel for the rest of the week so you wouldn't be embarrassed, but this is more private. In a hotel, people might see us together, or gossip if they saw Cyril in the same hotel. This is much safer for me, and my future, don't you think, Calista? It's only for a week. I think a week should be enough to conceive, don't you?"

"I've absolutely no idea. After two inseminations and an accidental pregnancy, I'm the last person to give you advice."

"You are so funny. I love your sense of humour." She turned at the doorway. "Let's go shopping today. The little lady who makes my frocks has silk fabric, just arrived from Australia. Someone found a warehouse with bolts of fabric. The ship came into Lyttleton a week ago and I have first choice. We may not get another chance, ever. Come with me. I'll buy you a frock."

Calista lifted the sleeping baby over her shoulder and stood. "And where would I wear a silk dress? I'll come with you for the company. We can leave the babies in the crèche, but I'll need to be back by mid-afternoon when the children return from school." Her spirit lifted with the thought of a girls' day out. Josephine had both the energy and the money to make things happen. It would be a nice change from administration and nursing. Dr Webb could cope for a day without her, and admin never went bad from neglect. It would be there tomorrow, waiting for attention.

With Jessica tucked into her cot, she returned to bed and snuggled against Mathew. He turned and kissed her, wrapping her in a hug, murmuring his love in her ear, but she didn't sleep. Her mind kept returning to the machinations Josephine seemed mired in. Perhaps her life was relatively simple in comparison.

Chapter 17

A month later, Calista arrived home from collecting the children to find Josephine's trap in the courtyard and her pony presumably stabled already. A quick check with Benjamin confirmed Josephine had arrived a short while ago and was apparently in the house.

Caleb and Vanily ran ahead looking for Connor, and Jessica toddled after them, still unable to move at speed, although her desire to climb things hadn't eased as she'd learned to walk.

Calista found Josephine in the lounge with Connor, and their conversation murmured along beneath the high-pitched chatter of the children.

"How long are you up for?" Calista asked.

"Just a few days this time. I told Castor I needed to talk to Peter Tonkin and Daphne about their wedding at the farm six weeks from now. Dot a few *i*'s and cross a few *t*'s." Josephine grinned.

"I thought things were sorted. Daphne seems to think so. She has her dress, and they're going to remain living in the boarding house with the Fletchers until Peter builds them a house."

"Of course things are sorted." Josephine giggled and flicked her hand at Calista. "You are so slow, Calista. I had other reasons. Surely you can think of another reason I'm here?"

"Not Cyril again?"

"Of course, I think we've hit the jackpot already, but I just thought I'd make doubly sure."

"You are incorrigible, you really are," said Calista, but she couldn't suppress a smile.

"I have an appointment to see Dr Elizabeth before I go home. She can confirm I'm pregnant, but just in case I'm not, I thought

I could keep trying." She smiled. "And I can tell Castor my news when I get home. He'll be so happy."

"And so will I," Calista said. "Your nighttime antics weigh heavy on my heart."

"Oh, don't be so dramatic, Callie. You are so serious at times. Try and enjoy life a bit more."

"With you as a friend, my life is never dull." She stood. "Shall we leave the children playing? I have to start on the evening meal, it's my turn tonight. You can help. It'll be a novel experience for you, seeing as you have Mrs Rasmussen doing all your meals. I wouldn't want you to forget how to boil an egg."

"Now you are bordering on being rude. Of course I'll help get dinner. I brought a side of lamb as my contribution to housekeeping. It's in the chiller room."

"Wonderful, I'll put a leg on for dinner. The men will be delighted. Your farm lamb is so delicious."

Once the vegetables were prepared, the children lined up around the table for an early meal. With the smell of roasting lamb wafting through the house, Calista poured herself and Josephine a glass of honey mead. They sipped their drinks and fed their toddlers.

"What's news at the farm, other than wedding preparations? Any gossip?" Calista aimed another spoonful at Jessica's mouth between the child's efforts to feed herself.

"Yes, I meant to tell you. Remember those two men you pointed out to me? The ones Will Jasper had Cyril take to Timaru? The ones that kidnapped you?"

"As if I'll ever forget them! Why?"

"They turned up recently with a written request from the Dome Council, requisitioning produce from us. Can you believe that? Demanding their requirements be given priority over all our crops and produce—payment guaranteed."

"What?" Calista's heart dropped. This would affect their supplies from the farm. It would be disastrous if Castor complied.

"Don't worry. Castor gave them short shrift. The two men, Charleston and Biggs, were watched every moment they were on the premises. Will Jasper detests them. Castor wrote a formal reply saying he would add the Dome Council to our customer base and inform them by radio telephone of any surplus we had, but he did not intend to disenfranchise his existing loyal customers, all of whom also paid promptly."

"But how did they know about your farm, to even send the request."

"From Charleston and Biggs—and Wallace Howe, I guess."

"How would Wallace know? He's never been there."

"Yes, he has. He came with Cyril on the first trip south to Timaru and they stayed the night." She lifted Connor out of the highchair and sat him on the floor. "Cyril called in to see what we had that he could cart on a regular basis, which he now does every trip. It's a detour but worth his while, and a great service to the farm. It saves us sending a wagon and driver there and back. Howe would have seen a lot of the farm's operation in the time he was there: the paddocks of vegetables, the orchard, the dairy sheds, the beef cattle...not to mention the endless fields of wheat."

"The waterwheel-driven flour mill," Calista added, her favourite thing to watch.

"And the tall silos that dry the grain harvest. We're not visible from the main highway, but once you travel in past the coastal hills, it's flat for miles and they're a landmark, along with the house."

"Do you think the Dome Council will accept Castor's refusal?" Calista swallowed a thread of fear. "I heard the other day from a patient at the clinic that people were starting to drift north from Queenstown. The Skydome was fractured so badly by the earthquakes the climate is reverting to what it was before they built it. There's heavy snow on the Remarkable Range and cold winds and sleet leaking in. The hothouse effect has gone and food is becoming short." She paused before asking, "Does Castor know this is happening in Queenstown and Wanaka?"

Josephine grimaced. "Yes, we've heard the same but we're trying not to worry. We've had a few stragglers arrive and Jasper has taken on more men. They have to be strong and willing to work. Our accommodation block is full, except for the family bunk block which we are keeping empty for guests." She smiled. "The Carbonites and their friends will all be housed for the wedding but after that, we might have to use them for the autumn harvest." She reached for the bottle and refilled their glasses. "I hope the trickle of Dome refugees doesn't become a flood. We're hoping they'll keep to the coast road and not find us."

Once the children were finished, they gathered up the empty

plates and took the two small children to the bathroom to settle them early. Caleb and Vanily returned to the toys in the lounge.

While they watched the toddlers splashing in the bath they continued their discussion. "After dinner, I'd like you to talk to the men. They need to know this wave of refugees is coming. It's serious when the Dome Council tries to exert pressure on the outside world. They've managed to ignore us decades," Calista said. "Things must be bad for them to even consider it."

Josephine lifted Connor out of the bath and onto a towel. "I suspect they're trying to retain a grip on the population. Wallace Howe has probably used his knowledge of our operations to further his climb up the hierarchy."

"They're heartless," Calista said. "I've experienced their lack of humanity. They'll stop at nothing to retain their authority, and now that the tunnel communities have been destroyed and the railway lines blocked, the other thing they'll be short of is coal. The trains used to carry coal from Arthur's Pass to Wanaka daily." The image of people freezing in the winter chill made her shudder. "It will be worse once winter hits. People will die."

"I know. We've discussed this at the farm. Castor is thinking of digging bunkers into the one hillside we have and storing some food there, hidden by grass-covered doors. It's only an idea but we might have to do it. Until the refugee population sorts itself out we could be overrun by starving souls. We can't feed everyone."

"What flows north past you will arrive here." Calista chewed her lip as she dried Jessica. The enormity of the looming disaster frightened her. They would probably be safe within the stockade, but the demand for bread and medicines would be overwhelming. Would they cope? How could anybody cope?

Where would these poor refugees sleep and live? In the empty, broken concrete structures, the old car parking buildings that everyone else avoided? There would be no shortage of work for anyone. More houses could be built. The portable sawmills were already working overtime producing timber from the beech and pine forests. There was no shortage of wood. No shortage of coal, either, as long as you were prepared to cart it from Arthur's Pass. Mathew, Kyle and Winston had been carting coal for weeks, getting ready for the winter and stockpiling it in high fenced depots—not that a high fence would stop a determined thief.

She and Mary already baked bread twice a week. Could they manage another day—or would that depend on the supply of flour from the farm? And the clinic would be overrun with people needing help. They'd need security to protect their medical supplies and Dr Elizabeth's rooms.

She couldn't solve this. The ball of ice in her chest would slowly melt once her worries were passed on to the men. The Carbonites would make decisions and action any plans. This is when they shone: in a crisis or an emergency. They'd probably quite enjoy the urgency and the tension. She wondered if it harked back to caveman days when men had to go out and slay a mammoth or two. Problems seemed to energise men, but all this did was mire her in worry.

The excitement of Josephine's arrival was dulled by her news. What they'd suspected might be happening further south had been confirmed by the Dome Council's demands.

Damn them and damn Wallace Howe. When would he get out of her life?

Josephine broke into her sombre thoughts: "I thought I might ask Dr Elizabeth to the wedding. Do you think she'd come?"

"Probably, as long as you assure her she won't have to check out the health of all your workers while she's there."

"I wouldn't expect her to. Why do you say that?"

"Because a lot of people do that to doctors, and I've seen it happen to Elizabeth," Calista hitched Jessica onto her hip but stopped at the doorway. "Who's going to marry Peter and Daphne?"

"Castor thought he might get permission from the Court and do it, but it seems that the couple have already arranged a marriage celebrant that Cyril introduced them to. He was a passenger on one of Cyril's trips."

"He's a man of many parts, your Cyril, isn't he?"

Josephine stood from kneeling beside the bath and stepped forward. She held Calista's gaze, her expression serious and her eyes flashing ice-green. "He's a hardworking, loyal man, Calista. He adores you and your crazy Carbonite band. He is honest as the day is long and provides a service that helps a lot of people. More people than you are aware of, many of them travel free." She grasped Calista's arm. "I don't dally with him without good reason. He is doing me a great favour and I am trusting him with my life.

I do not love him. I'm using his genes and we both know it. Please don't disparage him because he has agreed to help consolidate my marriage and a future for all of us, including the Carbonites.

"Castor wants a dynasty and I intend to provide him with one, however I can." Her grasp tightened. "I need you, Calista. I value your friendship. I will support you any way I can, providing you continue to support me." She smiled, her gaze softened. "Friends?" she asked.

With Jessica on her hip and only one arm free, Calista hugged her in response. "Of course, I didn't mean to offend you. I was only teasing but it obviously hit a nerve. I'm sorry. I won't mention it again."

"Thank you, and I'll make sure when I invite Elizabeth to the wedding that she knows it's a purely social invitation. I'm hoping she will deliver my next child, so there's method in my madness."

Six weeks had passed since Josephine's visit and the fears her news had triggered were now under control. The Carbonites would handle it. Calista sighed, and a sense of happiness warmed her as she gazed over the orchard. Nothing like a wedding to chase away the blues. The trees were laden with fruit and the branches festooned with decorations. The farm children had been busy with paper, pastels and finger paint. Ribbons hung from branches and small stars swirled and twisted in the breeze. The long trestles, covered in white linen cloths, were now scattered with leftovers from the wedding breakfast. The men were collecting up the plates and cutlery and taking them away to wash. The women were sitting around in chairs, watching the children and sipping their alcoholic drinks. Their contribution to the wedding had been in the preparation, and Will Jasper had organised the men to do the clearing up.

Everyone who worked on the farm had been invited, as guests. The whole day had been a celebration of being alive and the marriage represented hope for the future. Tonight Peter and Daphne would share a double bunk bed, instead of squeezing into a single bunk as everyone knew they had been up to until now. There were no secrets in the family quarters. Daphne looked glorious in a frock Josephine had bought her. Mrs Rasmussen had beamed with pride, and Mathew and Calista had stood in as Peter's parents. There'd been moments of sadness with the toast to absent friends, but Mathew put his arm around Peter's shoulders and held him close. The moment had passed and joy had won the day.

To think she'd once been frightened to arrive at the farm. She thought of her first visit, when Castor had flirted and wanted to marry her then and there, fresh out of the tunnels. She'd been so frightened, but Father had whisked her away in the dawn light, keeping her safe, not wanting to offend Castor. Now she had a better understanding of how important the farm was to the Carbonites. On her second arrival at the farm, when she and Mathew had escaped the tunnels, she'd been scared again of Castor's plans, but he'd married—and now Josephine, who'd been so haughty and regal, considered her as a friend. Life was full of twists and turns.

This visit to the farm promised to be pure joy and delight. The bevy of children ran through the trees in a never-ending game of chasey. Their piping voices interrupted the music from an old squeezebox someone was playing back at the house. Pure bliss. No one needed her, no one had a job for her to do or a question to answer; nothing to stitch up, no accounts to balance and tomorrow promised to be another glorious day.

Beside her, Elizabeth dozed, an empty glass standing in the grass beside her chair. The lines around her eyes had eased a little and she looked less stressed. It had worked out well. Elizabeth made her potions and helped Dr Webb in the clinic one day a week. Her remedies were popular and the demand for them grew. Elizabeth had said in the spring she'd need to pick more leaves, and by then Calista was planning to go with her; not that anyone knew of this, not even Elizabeth.

If she couldn't be a doctor, she'd be a doctor's assistant.

Chapter 18

She couldn't sleep. After tossing for hours, Calista decided it was either too much honey mead, a day of excitement or the moonlight shining in the window of the family quarters. Something was keeping her awake and Mathew's gentle snoring and the snuffles of her three children only made her sleeplessness more annoying. She might as well get up and go for a walk. It was light enough by the moon and she knew her way to the mill and the waterwheel, somewhere she loved, and to sit alone there would be a luxury.

Slipping on her shoes, she pulled her cloak around her shoulders. It would keep her warm no matter what the temperature and would stretch long enough to sit on by the riverbank. The moonlight glistened on the dew dusting the grass beside the farm track. She walked past the barn where the horses slept, her footsteps crunching where potholes had been filled with shell and sand. A horse snickered to her and her cloak swished through the grass when she turned off the track and made her way through the riverside trees to the edge of the stream. While her feet were chilled, the rest of her stayed cosy. The moonlight danced on the water coming over the wheel and, with no flour being ground this weekend, the wheel rolled without restriction to the speed of the water.

Lulled by the sound, her mind wandered over past events and her present life. Nothing to complain about: healthy children, a loving husband, good friends. An abundance of luck seemed to have blessed them all.

The sound of voices whispering nearby made her stiffen. *Farm residents would not be whispering!*. All were asleep after a day of feasting and celebrating Peter and Daphne's wedding vows. The murmuring grew closer, and then came the squeak of wood protesting as if being forced apart. Thieves? A hungry refugee? Had word that the farm's abundance of food was here for the taking spread southward? She moved with studied slowness, rising to her feet, stepping to the shadow of the largest tree, and listened.

The sound of something dropping onto wood, followed by cursing and then a demand to hush, confirmed her suspicions. Robbers, and more than one. How many she didn't know but it seemed they were breaking into the grinding room on the other side of the building. There would be some bags of flour there, she knew, but most would be stored elsewhere. Nearby were the large sheds where the surplus vegetables and fruit were stacked, cool and dry, along with a few pumpkins, barely ripe but good enough to make pumpkin pies for the wedding and to roast in the fire beside the lamb on the spit.

Footsteps nearby had fear racing like ice through her body. She stiffened and so did her cloak. Would she be seen in the shadows? Her cloak was dark but her hair and face were exposed.

"A woman. I see a woman, here in the trees," a husky male voice called out.

Too late now to conceal herself, she grasped her cloak together at her neck and ran back toward the accommodation bunkhouses. Someone pulled at her cloak but it slipped out of their grasp, almost falling off her shoulders, but she clung tight, holding it to her chest, her thumb pressing the button on the back of her pendant, alerting the Carbonites she was in danger. She twisted her head to see the flash of a knife in the moonlight and felt it snag her cloak, bruising her arm, but the blade didn't penetrate the cloth. Her cloak had sensed her fear and hardened. She ran faster, knowing the way, dodging around obstacles she knew were there despite not being able to see them clearly. Her footsteps were confident despite her haste. An oath was shouted behind her and the sound of a stumble, followed by a thud, confirmed her pursuer had hit the ground. She didn't look back to check. Terror drove her onward.

The sound of pursuit ceased and with the pain of a stitch in her side she stumbled, then righted herself with her thumb constantly pressed against her pendant. Surely someone would come. In front of her a man appeared, large and tall—Winston—and she gasped: "Thieves at the mill...breaking down doors. Three, I heard, probably more."

Behind him Mathew arrived, then Peter Tonkin, then her father tucking his shirt into his trousers. Simon arrived, smelling of horse, bits of hay in his sparse hair. He must have been sleeping near his beloved horses—and then Benjamin arrived, last, from the direction of the house. Perhaps he was more than just friends with Mrs Rasmussen?

She brushed off queries of her safety and pointed down the track. The men turned as a group toward the mill and she hissed, "They have knives, be careful." This halted them and they ran past her into the vegetable gardens. Were they mad? "Wrong way, that way," she called after them but they ignored her.

Mathew turned back and held her close, questioning her again. "What are you doing out here? It's dangerous. I think you should go to the house. Now. Please, Calista." He had his Kempo fighting stick grasped tight.

"I'm fine, truly. I was sitting, watching the waterwheel—couldn't sleep—when I heard them. One of them tried to catch me but I left him behind. My cloak saved me."

He stroked its surface. "It's hard, like stiff leather."

"The memory thread must have sensed my fear. The knife didn't penetrate."

They both turned to watch the Carbonites returning from the gardens, each holding a stake or pole. Of course, it hadn't occurred to her before: Winston would have taught all of them Kempo, not just Mathew. All except for Peter, who ignored her father's shouted order to stay back and trailed behind them, carrying his garden stake as if it were a flagstaff. She feared he might get injured—or worse—and yet there he was, a young man on his wedding night, prepared to use a stick to defend his community against men with knives.

Her stomach roiled at the danger they were racing toward. She watched Mathew's back as he disappeared into the darkness. *Please, Zeus, keep him safe.* At that moment she realised how much she loved him.

She jumped in fright as Will Jasper stepped out of the gloom and stood beside her.

"Miss Calista, could you man the siren for me? It will get all my men out of bed." Despite the urgency, his request was courteous, as if she might refuse. She followed him as he ran toward his office.

He turned the handle on an apparatus mounted on the side of the building. A wail split the darkness like an axe. She resisted the urge to put her fingers in her ears. He pointed and said, "Here, take over. Keep winding. This is our security alarm." He looked around. "How many do you reckon?"

"I don't know," she shouted over the noise of the alarm, "but definitely three at the flour mill, and there's all the other food storage buildings they could be breaking into." The siren continued to wail, rising and falling as she turned the handle, a hideous noise that would surely wake every living creature for miles around.

Will stepped close and cupped his hand around her ear so she could hear him say, "As each man arrives, tell him what you think is happening and send him toward the mill. Perhaps send a couple to the orchard, and some to the food stores. Can you do that?"

Of course she could. She nodded.

"But they will be unarmed," she shouted in his ear. "The thieves have knives. One of them tried to stab me." Just the memory made her want to retch.

"My men will have grabbed rakes, sticks, crowbars, whatever they have nearby. We've practised for such an event. I can't stand here and give you the details. Trust me."

"Sorry, Will."

He patted her shoulder. "You're doing a great job. Just keep the alarm screaming." And suddenly he was gone, racing away into the darkness. A moment later a worker stumbled toward her, eyes bleary with sleep, trousers barely held up, and a thick axe handle in his hand.

"Robbers, at the mill and the food stores. They have knives," she shouted.

He disappeared and others arrived. She issued instructions, spreading their placement as Will had asked. They all carried a weapon of some sort and if it hadn't been such a serious moment she'd have thought that some of their weapons were amusing; a horsewhip, a steel frying pan, a hammer, a small wooden ladder and the strut of a clothesline prop, a V cut in one end so it could be used to hold up the fence wire to allow men through—and sticks, many sticks, with vicious, pointed ends.

Both her arms ached, alternating which one she used, her spare hand blocking an ear. At last, the stream of men ceased. Should she stop winding the siren now?

The moon remained hidden behind the clouds and through the dark Cyril appeared, frightening her with his sudden appearance. She jumped, a brief squeal escaping unintended. Like a dog stalking a rabbit, he'd arrived without any sound, or else the siren had masked his approach.

He gave her a brief hug and chuckled. "It's alright, Calista, only me. I've just made sure Daphne and Pelly have all the children in the big house, and I had to go to my wagon to get my weapon from the lock-up cupboard. Which way should I go?"

"I've no idea," she said. The sounds of men grunting, weapons clashing and voices cursing reached them from the coal-black dark. Not close enough to put her or anyone in the big house in danger but frightening to listen to. More light would be useful—and as if to answer her wish, the moon popped out from behind a cloud, revealing the fight scene in front of them. Not as far away as she'd thought. Dangerously close.

"Time you got into the house. All the men will have mustered by now. By the number of women and children at the big house, they have all left their houses and have gathered in the ballroom, as planned. Good to know the security drills have worked."

He knew about the security drills? What else did this man have his fingers in? Glad to be rid of the noise, she dropped the handle and let the siren's wail fade and then set off toward the house, her ears ringing. She turned briefly to see Cyril, his tall, solid frame standing, legs akimbo like a tripod and his arm raised high toward the sky.

Then a shot rang out and the fight scene turned into a tableau lit by the moon, as if everyone was playing a game of statues.

A gun!

The gunshot made Winston stop and take a deep breath. Sounded like a real bullet. With a gun in the mix, their fight had ramped up a step from knives and batons. Who had the gun?

Cyril's voice rang out as loud as the gunshot, cutting through the grunts and gasps of the fighting men. "Drop your weapons. Stop fighting. We won't kill you. If you're hungry we will feed you. If you've come to steal from us, then negotiation is the better course to follow."

Winston looked at the man at his feet. He'd just disarmed him with a blow to the back of his knees, causing the man to slam backward onto the ground. He appeared winded, his hands fluttering at his side. He no longer presented a threat, and Winston pushed him onto his side. He'd probably get his breath back in a few minutes, but Winston kept his boot on the man in case he decided to get up.

One of the attackers challenged Cyril's request. "I don't believe you. Once we drop our weapons you can attack us again." The ragged voice came from the back of the mob. Another joined in, "Yeah, can't trust outsiders. You're all addle-brained with radiation."

No one moved.

"Then we're fighting well for people with addled brains, aren't we?" No one contradicted Cyril. "We're organised and you're outnumbered. If you fight on you'll be injured and disarmed. How will you return home, wherever that is, and how will you carry your stolen loot if you are maimed or crippled?"

A mumble of voices grew in volume until a voice shouted, "One last stand, men. Let's not give up what we've fought for."

"Ignore him," Cyril commanded. "I'm the one with the gun and I'll shoot to kill the next man who attacks."

A long silence followed until the soft thud of weapons hitting the ground triggered a collective sigh and the tension broke like the silent snap of a worn rubber band. A low curse, followed by another thud, began a rain of clunks as the attackers laid down their arms.

"Thank you," Cyril said, his tone level and calm. "If you will line up against the wall of the food store, we will check you for concealed knives and then you will be offered food, and we will discuss how you can leave and return to wherever you came from." There were a few snarled asides and mutterings of disbelief. "If you have friends you know are injured, please go and stand next to them so we can get them attended to." A few shadows moved across the scene as men stepped through the grass, calling softly to each other, checking their mates' whereabouts.

Winston watched, impressed with Cyril's command of the situation. Hadn't he been a guard at one of the tunnel exits? Guess he must have learned mob control in his training. But where had he got the gun? Then he remembered Mathew's account of their arrival back at the base of the mountain after searching the tunnels, and the two scouts who'd menaced the crowd and waved a gun about. Cyril had stepped up with Mathew to face down the men and disarm them. He must have ended up with the gun—and some bullets.

Cyril was probably the best man to have the weapon, even if it was illegal to own bullets. Having a loaded gun was probably a necessity with his cartage business. Sometimes he must transport dubious people and precious goods—like food. What a tragedy that men were now fighting each other over food. Times were getting harder every year and the earthquakes hadn't helped.

Peter Tonkin joined him, standing beside him, his stick upright, looking unused.

"What's the groom of the day doing out here?" Mathew ask. "You had other priorities tonight."

The young man smiled and ducked his head, embarrassed. "Cyril told me off as well, made me stand at the back of the melee. Said I had to watch and let him know if anyone sneaked through toward the big house."

"Quite right, you've not had enough Kempo lessons yet to defend yourself. These intruders meant business." He nodded toward the lineup. "A few extra knives being found, I see. Nasty things, knives, no memories. Don't know what not to cut."

The man at his feet groaned and sat up. Winston bent down and offered his hand, pulling the man to his feet and holding him steady.

"Dad?" Peter's voice hitched. "Dad, is that you?" He looked at Winston, his voice edged with disbelief. "It's my father, Rufus. I can't believe he's alive. I thought he'd died in the tunnels."

The man staggered and shook his head. "Must be dreaming. Must've hit my head." He knuckled his ears. "I keep hearing my son's voice."

"Dad! It's me, Peter. What are you doing here? You're alive? Is Mum alive?"

The young man threw himself into the arms of his father and they rocked each other. Winston stood nearby, ready to catch them if they fell. Their cries of joy and loss rent the night air in the moments of their reunion. A wonderful wedding present for Peter, tinged with sadness by the slow shake of Rufus Tonkin's head to Peter's queries about his mother.

"Take your father up to the big house, son, and let them know the fight is over." He patted Peter on the head and gripped Rufus Tonkin's shoulder in a brief acknowledgement of comradeship. "I'll go and help Cyril and Aaron and see what we're going to do with the injured—and the hungry." As an afterthought, he turned back to them. "Better tell Dr Elizabeth her skills might be needed, would you, Peter?"

The groom of the day grinned, delight lighting his face, his cheeks wet in the moonlight. "I need to introduce Dad to my wife too, don't I, Dad?"

Rufus Tonkin straightened his back with obvious effort and under the ragged clothes, the dishevelled hair and tangled beard, Winston saw hope on the face of a man who'd just found his family and a reason to look forward to the future.

"Lead on, Peter. I'd love to meet my daughter-in-law."

Winston walked toward the food store where lanterns had been lit, and some of the late peach crop were being handed out to the prisoners. Their bemused expressions were reward enough. A group of farmworkers had lit a rudimentary cooking station and were heating water for tea. The smell of lamb chops being seared wafted on the night air, making Winston's mouth water even though he was well-fed. Surely it would hearten the defeated? Other farmworkers were tending the wounded and Aaron was talking to what appeared to be the leader of the rag-tag bunch of a dozen thieves. A shout of recognition rang out as one of the farmhands recognized a previous tunnel neighbour and their playful teasing of each other further eased the tension.

At Aaron's side, Winston said, "This is just the beginning, Master Aaron, don't you think?"

"I'm afraid so, although how we're going to cope with the refugees from the Dome, I don't know." He rubbed his arm and Winston saw blood had soaked his shirt sleeve.

"Injured?"

"A slice from a knife. I'll have to get my daughter to sew me up. I hear she's very handy with a needle and thread."

"And with a siren, according to Jasper. If she hadn't been out in the moonlight we might have woken to ransacked food stores and no flour left by morning." He reached and took a strip of torn fabric from the bundle in the hands of a passing worker and tied a tourniquet around Aaron's arm. "She's a good lass. Worth her weight in gold—or flour," he added with a smile.

"She is. Even if she's a bit stroppy at times, she's a good daughter."

"Might pay to tell her that occasionally, if you don't mind me saying."

Aaron Waterman sucked his teeth for a moment, his gaze drifting over the men gathered around them and Winston wondered if he'd overstepped the bounds of their friendship, then Aaron grasped his hand and squeezed it.

"You are quite right, Winston. She's a true Carbonite, and I shall tell her so. And I'll say it to her more often from now on."

Chapter 19

The dawn light crept across the landscape, drawing ever closer, revealing the buildings standing weary on their footings. The worn weatherboards mimicked the tiredness in Calista's body. She'd been awake for hours and her bones were demanding rest, even as a rooster crowed, alerting the world to the coming day.

She and Elizabeth had worked since the surrender. The hungry mob from the south had incurred a few broken limbs to be set because sticks wielded by the Carbonites and the various other weapons in the hands of the farm's workers had inflicted a lot of damage. No one died, but there were two cases of concussion and a dozen or so with wounds to be stitched together. Even her father had stood at the end of the line, "awaiting my daughter's handwork", he'd joked, although in the dim electric light his pale complexion and the sweat beaded on his forehead revealed his pain. The solar panel batteries were a godsend at times like this. She'd done her best and hoped the scars would heal without ending up pronounced and ugly.

Elizabeth had triaged everyone and had them lined up in order of urgency. The broken bones had required copious quantities of alcohol to deaden the men's senses, and crutches would be in order for the next few weeks. The single men's accommodation block now doubled as a recovery ward and Elizabeth had agreed to stay on for a few days and return with Cyril on his next trip north.

Discussions with the injured invaders revealed some had wives and children hidden nearby and Kyle volunteered to leave in the morning with a wagon, along with several uninjured men, to convince the women and children to come to the farm for food and comfort.

"Penny for them?" Mathew slid his arm around her waist, and she leaned her head on his shoulder.

"All I truly want to do is to go to sleep. Who would imagine that a walk in the moonlight would result in me being up for the rest of the night?" She rubbed her eyes. The long hours of peering at wounds in half-light had made them sore.

"Just as well you couldn't sleep. Where would we all be now if you hadn't heard the intruders?"

"We'd be just waking up, and although there'd be less food in the stores, no one would have been hurt." She looked up at him, taking in his tired gaze, the lines at the corners of his eyes and the beginning of a beard around his jaw. "I'm so glad you weren't injured. My heart sank as you walked into the melee in the dark." Her eyes prickled and she fought the ache in her throat. "I was so frightened you'd be injured—or worse, killed."

"I wouldn't put myself in that much danger. I'm able to defend myself quite well." He looked into the distance where the light had finally arrived on the first dustings of snow on the Southern Alps. "It wasn't as dangerous as going into the tunnels after the earthquake. That was terrifying."

"You never talk about that day." She slipped around to snuggle into his chest, inhaling his essence, his *Mathewness* that made her feel secure.

"It's hard to talk about it, and talking about it won't change anything. Mass destruction is messy, smelly, and like a glimpse into hell. If such a place exists then that's what it must be like."

She took his hand and pulled him along. "Come on, let's go to bed. Someone will look after the children when they wake up, surely." As they strolled toward the accommodation block, she wondered aloud, "It must have affected Peter as much as you, yet he never mentions it either."

"He does to me, but now his father is here he'll have the parental support he needs. He's matured into a fine young man. He's a bit young to be married, but these days it seems to be the norm."

"Here I am with three children, and just about to turn twenty-one. I can't judge Peter and Daphne wanting to be together."

"But yours wasn't a life choice."

"No, except for Jessica, but I wouldn't part with any of them."

"Neither would I," Mathew said. "Let's creep in quietly and

hope they don't wake up."

By midday, those awake in the night had snatched a few hours' sleep and once more the tables in the orchard were covered in food. A picnic atmosphere prevailed. The injured were sitting around on bales of hay, farmworkers mingling with the night's intruders, children racing between the adults, and a pleasant hum of conversation soothed any tension between the two groups.

Castor Seville walked to the front of the group and tapped a crystal glass with a silver spoon. The clear ring broke through the chatter and silence descended. All gazes turned to the Squire. This was his farm, his fiefdom, and they were all sharing his hospitality. Respect was required.

However, from the grin on his face he was pleased about something. He beckoned Josephine to stand beside him, and once he had his arm around her waist he cleared his throat and began.

"I have an announcement to make. To add to the joy of seeing Mrs Rasmussen's daughter Daphne married to Peter Tonkin yesterday, I'd like to share our news. My wife and I are expecting our second child, due to arrive before Christmas, a playmate for Connor."

Cheers sounded with calls of "Congratulations, Squire", and Calista noted that Josephine blushed and tried to look embarrassed by the whole occasion. She was a good actress, but in all fairness, her plan to keep Castor happy and the farm's future secure had worked. It crossed Calista's mind that things could get a bit tricky in the future if Castor required more children. But then again, it had worked so far and Cyril cheered and whooped along with everyone else, so he would no doubt be happy to continue with the arrangement, if required. What did it matter? They were hurting no one. If anything, their arrangement seemed to be causing much joy. Plus it could be Castor's child after all.

"To my good friends, the Carbonites, thank you," Castor continued. "Without your early intervention last night we may have been still fighting this morning, or waking to find our larder plundered." He waited for the confirming comments to fade, then added, "To our injured guests: you can stay here and work for me, or you can leave to find work and food elsewhere. I ask one favour. Do not spread your knowledge of our location and our food supplies. We work this farm to feed ourselves and all surpluses go to feed others. The Carbonites do their best to spread assistance and sustenance. I'm happy to continue to give them our leftovers. The produce we sell and trade goes in all directions and feeds many, but if we are plundered and attacked we will be forced to defend ourselves and our generosity will cease."

Someone in the crowd stood and raised his glass. "A toast to the Squire and his good lady. Good health and long legs to the baby." This version of a toast raised a few chuckles and then everyone clapped.

"Eat up and be merry, because tomorrow we work," Will Jasper said. His comment was followed by a lot of good-natured groans. Calista stretched to grasp Mathew's hand and squeezed it.

"Life's pretty good, isn't it, sweetheart?" he murmured in her ear, and she smiled and kissed his cheek, hoping he would shave sometime soon.

"Home tomorrow, and back to work for us as well," she replied, and wondered when she should tell him about Elizabeth's invitation to go on a foraging trip in the spring into the bush behind Cheviot. Just the thought of it made her heart race. The anticipation of such a trip would carry her through the coming winter months. By then she'd have worked out how to spread her workload to others.

Her gaze drifted to take in their surroundings. Any residual fear she'd had of the farm had disappeared, well and truly banished. The farm now represented a source of goodness, a place where life began and fresh dreams were imagined. The impressions of last night; the fear, the noise of men fighting, the smell of sweat, and blood seeping from wounds, were fading as the sun washed her memory clean, giving a brighter edge to the remembered darkness. Even the dimness of her life in the tunnels had taken on a warmer glow—not that she would ever want to return to that life.

She looked for and found her children, numbered them off: one, two, three, then leaned back in her chair and closed her eyes. Sleep beckoned once more as she listened to the sounds around her: children playing, adults talking, someone tuning a fiddle in the distance and closer still a bee nearby, then the plop of an apple falling from the tree they sat under.

Tonight was another celebration, her birthday; twenty-one years old, officially an adult responsible for all her actions. Hadn't she always been? No, only in the past three years had she had the freedom she'd always desired.

In Angela's kitchen, the dining table was covered with a precious, old white linen tablecloth, the best cutlery and napkins gracing each place setting. The mixed cutlery didn't matter, nor the mismatched crockery. Earthquakes had wrecked many a dinner set in the past years but Angela had inherited enough to make a beautiful setting. Fresh flowers sat in a vase in the table centre, obviously picked by the children because they contained daisies, oxalis, and wildflowers from by the river. Each bloom was a gift of love, picked with serious consideration and placed along with the roses from Angela's garden.

Tonight her father had shaved his beard off, his jaw and chin pale against the rest of his face, but his eyes sparkled and he looked younger than Calista could remember. Worry lines had been wiped from his face and he stood tall. He'd even put on some weight. They both knew his life had become much simpler since Eleanor's death, but no one mentioned it. He and Angela had formalised their union at the Court, with her and Mathew as witnesses and now everyone was getting on with everyday living.

Her father beckoned and she left the kitchen and followed him into the lounge. Small glasses sat on an occasional table, filled with something golden. Whisky? Honey mead? Bound to be alcoholic, no doubt, and Aaron passed them a glass each. The children all had glasses of juice and were standing in a solemn row, ready for the toast. Even Jessica managed to stand still for a brief moment, then she lost interest and sat down to play with a toy.

"I'd like to propose a toast to my daughter," Aaron said, looking to Mathew, Angela and Calista. "To my firstborn, to the child whose welfare kept me plotting, waiting for the years to pass until she was old enough to be liberated." He turned to her and held her gaze. "You are a constant source of joy to me, and even when we don't see eye to eye, I always know you're striving for a goal that sometimes only you can see. You've given me grandchildren and by marrying Mathew you have made him legally the son he has been to me for the past few years." His eyes glistened and he wiped one corner with the back of his free hand. "You are a good and kind daughter to Angela and I am so proud of you. Thank you for coming with me that day. Thank you for trusting me and having the courage to face a world you knew so little about. You are all a man could want in a daughter. You are loved by the men who follow me and my dreams." He raised his glass and said, "To Calista, my daughter, and a daughter to all the Carbonites."

What a long speech from her taciturn father. She sniffed, aware she too could shed a tear. She could reply and talk about her life in the tunnels. She could mention her mother and all she'd done for her and the children. She could thank her father for whisking her away from Castor Seville's attention and sending her to Cheviot, where she'd dallied with Mathew, experiencing love for the first time. She could mention her worries about the flood of people coming north and her idea to convert the old empty concrete parking buildings into accommodation, with internal dark rooms for those that needed them, as her mother had.

She could talk about what she'd learned since he'd led her out onto the ledge to look at the moon for the first time, and the revelations of life on the outside. Or talk about the simple pleasures she appreciated every day.

But she wouldn't do any of that.

Perhaps another time, in the future at another family celebration, she would give a speech and include the other Carbonites in her toast. At this moment she could only look around, take in the children, Colin, Belinda, Caleb, Vanily and Jessica, her darling Mathew; and Angela and her father…her family, her life.

Instead, she said, "Thank you, Father. Thank you for rescuing me and bringing me outside to live in the sun."